Melody's *song*

MEG FARRELL

ISBN-13: 978-0-9991278-2-7

Dedication

"Some souls just understand each other upon meeting."

~N.R. Hart

For those who have been there when things were ugly and seeing me through the trying times, Thank you.

(You know who you are. If I started listing people, I would forget someone, and they would be upset with me. If you think this is for you, it is!)

Acknowledgements

Cover design: Mignon Mykel of *Oh! So Novel*

http://ohsonovel.blogspot.com/

Editor: Victoria Miller

http://www.victoriamillerartist.com

Formatting: Bridgette O'Hare of *Dark Unicorn Designs*

http://www.darkunicorn.online

Chapter 1

Before

The rain falls rhythmically on the old tin roof covering the porch. This old porch is falling apart, but it's my safe place. I lie half-napping in the sway of the porch swing, trying not to think about what's happening inside the house, but it's proving to be almost impossible. Mama is in labor, trying to deliver my twin brothers. As per usual, my deadbeat father is drunk and passed out in his chair instead of helping. She's decided to have the babies at home, and Anna is here to help her. Anna is my mama's best friend who also happens to be a midwife. She's a sweet lady who always helps Mama with anything we need. She's much closer than any other friend of the family. I often call her Aunt Anna, but as I've grown up calling people "Aunt" or "Miss" seems childish, so now she's just Anna.

I worry about Mama and all the pain she's having, but Anna says the female body was designed by God and knows exactly what to do. The process, so far, causes me to doubt

Anna's firm beliefs. I don't dare voice my doubts because Anna would tear my tail up for not listening to her and having faith. My eyes roll involuntarily at the thought. I settle against the pillows on the swing and drift as I listen to the rain on the porch roof again.

While the rain is a relaxing, hypnotic distraction, I wish it would stop. It seems like it's been raining for months. The ground has been squishy for so long that I don't remember what it's like to walk without my feet slipping and sloshing inside my shoes. At least it's not cold. I can handle wet as long as it's not cold, too. It would be nice to take a walk and clear my mind without umbrellas, raincoats, and muddy boots. The smell of pine mixed with honeysuckle is probably my favorite combination when I've got a lot of thinking to do. Something about the sweet tang calms me. Maybe because we've lived in this same house, surrounded by these same trees, and the wild honeysuckle my entire life. The rain does work to trap more of the smells of the land around the house and everyone in it. For that, I'm thankful. The rain will only stay for a season, and I know it will pass. I heard on the news that we're two weeks from the official start of summer. Then I can be miserably hot instead of miserably wet.

Mama cries out, and I turn to look in through the screen door as she pauses her pacing. She's in the hallway outside the bedrooms, panting as she doubles over and scrunches her face together. I stand and the muscles in my legs flex as I start toward the door to help her, when Anna goes to her. She places her hand on Mama's back and leans down to her ear. Anna's hand moves in

2

circular motions on her back. After a few moments, Mama straightens up and begins pacing again.

Picking up my guitar, I sit back down on the porch swing and begin to play softly. I need to do something. Anything to help keep me on the porch instead of going inside and either getting in Anna's way or telling Dad what I really think about his lack of effort. I simply can't understand the relationship my parents have. Why does my Dad drink and sleep all day? Why does my mother continue breaking her back for him? And why, in God's name, would she get pregnant again? Anxiety builds in my chest thinking about all of the things I just don't understand, and I try to tamp it down by continuing to play.

The vibrations of the strings resonate through the body of the old, worn acoustic and into my hands. It's a primitive bond between instrument and player. One that I've enjoyed since I found the old girl in the attic several years ago. Moving my index, middle, and ring fingers into position for an A chord and strum. That chord was too tentative, so I strum the A chord again, and then move to the A7. This song is new to me, but I'm determined to play it well. I pick around the melody and strum all the right chords. I'm pretty impressed with myself when I hear my mother start singing a little from the house. the Beatles song, "Something," has always been one she sings while cooking, cleaning, or baking. When I was a very little girl, she would play her Beatles records all the time. It's one of my fondest memories.

Mama stops singing when another contraction starts. For the life of me, I don't know why Mama would chose to do this at home instead of going to the hospital like normal people. She told me we can't afford the hospital but don't hospitals have to help people? Even people without money? I've been worried about Mama for weeks. I even started reading on the Internet about high-risk pregnancies, and twins qualify as high-risk. All I know for sure is that reading about anything medical on the Internet is a mistake. On one website, Mama might die from complications. On the other website, they tout the responsibility of women to have the most natural birth possible. The Internet is absolutely impossible.

"Melody!" Anna calls.

"Coming!" I answer as I place my guitar on the porch swing so it won't fall over. I run inside the house to the back bedroom, and find that Anna's arms are covered in blood up to her elbows. Mama looks like she could be sleeping. But something doesn't feel right. There's no way she's sleeping. "What the…" But before I can finish, Anna cuts me off.

"Call an ambulance, Mel! Something's wrong!"

I can't move. My feet feel like concrete, and I can feel my heartbeat in my ears. *Why is there so much blood?* It's as if I'm watching a movie in slow motion. I look at Anna and her mouth is moving, but I can't hear her. All I can do is stand there. Something warm runs down my cheek and I'm crying.

Anna grabs me and shakes me out of the trance. "Melody! Call an ambulance! Now!" she shoves me back toward the living room.

"Okay," I say. My voice sounds so small. I manage to put my feet in motion and run for the phone. I dial 9-1-1, but when the operator answers, I can't get the words to come out of my mouth. I clear my throat and try again. "My mama is in labor and there's something wrong. We need help."

"Okay, honey." The operator tries to sound calming. "Where are you?"

"We're at home."

"Good. What's your address?"

"Oh!" I state, dumbly. "We live at 3425 County Road 46."

"You're doing great. What's your name, honey?"

"Melody."

"Melody, I'm Susan. You said your mama is in labor. How many weeks along is she?"

Weeks? "I don't know how many weeks," I state as I start crying harder. I sniffle. "She's like really pregnant. She's having twins. There is a ton of blood. Are you sending an ambulance?

Susan tries for calm again, "Stay on the line with me, okay? I have an ambulance dispatched. I need you to keep talking to me until they get there. Do you know if your mama has had any problems with this pregnancy?"

"I don't know," I answer immediately.

"All right, that's okay. Who is with your mama?"

5

"Her friend, Anna. She's a midwife."

"Anna Jones?" Susan asks.

"Yes. Anna Jones. She told me to call."

Susan sighs. "Okay. I know Anna. Your Mama is in good hands. She's delivered many babies in this county. Stay on the phone with me, Melody."

I don't say anything else as I wait for the ambulance to come. Anna is still buzzing around and checking Mama's pulse as I hold the phone like an idiot. Finally, I hear the sirens in the distance. Relief washes over me.

"Melody, the ambulance should almost be there. Do you hear them?"

My voice is thick when I say, "Yes."

Susan praises me, "Awesome. You did a good job, Melody. I hope everything goes well from here."

Frustrated with her calm and cheery disposition, I hang up the phone and immediately run to the living room to wake up my dad. "Daddy!" I yell, but he doesn't move. "*Daddy!* Get up! The babies are in trouble. We need you!" I start shaking him to try and get him to come around.

I run back into the bedroom. "Anna! What do I do? Can I help?"

Anna shakes her head. "There's nothing we can do."

Doors slam and I run to the porch to prop the screen door open for the paramedics. The first one is a large, grumpy looking man, and he bounds up the stairs with an orange bag in his hand and asks where he's going as he passes. I barely say "bedroom" loud enough for him to hear me. His partner is a young woman with a kind face. She retrieves a couple more packs from the back of the ambulance before coming inside. She's in less of hurry when she reaches me.

"Hey," she says gently with a small smile. "Are you okay?"

I nod. "It's my mama. She's in the back bedroom."

She pats my shoulder. "Wait here."

I am not about to stand here and wait. Wait for what? I follow them into the room, and the first paramedic is trying to revive my mama while Anna uses a stethoscope to see if she can hear the babies' heartbeats.

She looks up when she hears us. "Both babies still have a strong heartbeat, but I don't know for how long."

The man turns to the woman and says, "Mother's heartbeat is weak, respiration is low, and pulse ox is dwindling. She's lost a lot of blood."

Everything starts to spin out of control as they throw medical information at each other and keep working on Mama. At some point, the gurney is brought in, and my Mama is loaded up and rolled away. I'm not clear on everything that's happening, except for Anna giving me instructions.

"Melody you have to wake up your dad. He has to get to the hospital to make decisions."

I shake my head. "I don't know what to do."

Anna is stern, "Melody, your mama and I need you. The babies need you. Get your dad and get to the hospital."

"I can't drive. How are we supposed to get there?"

"You wake him up. Sunny is on his way to drive you. I have to go with her." She leaves me staring after her as she gets in the ambulance with Mama.

The doors are slammed closed, and then the ambulance takes off down the road. Panic rises in my throat because I have no idea how what to do. I'm lost. I need my mama. I can't do this. I'm starting to sob even more and can't catch my breath. But I can't sit here and cry about it. I have to do something to get to the hospital with Mama.

Anna's husband, Sunny, bursts through the front door. He ruffles my hair as he passes me. "Anna called me. Let's get your dad in the car and get to the hospital. All right, kiddo?" His voice booms when he speaks. I think he's probably got the deepest voice I've ever heard from anybody.

Sunny drives like a maniac in my parent's old boat of a station wagon. He's used to being alone on his humongous motorcycle, and I'm sure it's awkward for him to drive this dinosaur of a car. I wish there was something I could know or do to help. I'm scared to death. There's literally nothing for me to do.

8

Nothing.

We pull into the Emergency Room parking lot as they are taking Mama out of the back of the ambulance. Sunny is again helping to hold my Dad up as we walk into the hospital right behind them. The first person we see inside the Emergency Room is Anna. I'm relieved and run to her, throwing my arms around her neck. She holds me and hugs me back hard. Her hug is comforting. I don't want to let her go because she makes everything better. Reluctantly, I pull back and see the scowl on her face. She's staring at my dad as if she'd like to burn holes in him. She's as pissed about his inability to help in an urgent situation as I am.

Dad slumps into the waiting room chair that Sunny dumped him in. He drops his head in his hands. I don't know if he's praying or if the rush of adrenaline has killed his drunk. A tiny part of my heart aches for him. For the first time, I think he may not be fully aware of what's happening. *Am I?* He might lose his wife or his twin boys or both. I want to feel sorry for him and for myself. I can't because I'm so angry he can't help and that we are so broke that Mama thought she had to have the babies at home.

Anna interrupts. "Melody, your mama is still unconscious. The doctor has rushed her into surgery to try and deliver the babies. He thinks, once they get the babies out, they'll be able to figure out what's happening with your mama. It's going to be a little while. You should sit down."

"Mama's dying," I say. The words transform all of my anger into heartbreak as part of me shatters. A small, desperate noise escapes my lips as I sob, and Anna pulls me into her arms again.

"Shhh. Baby, we don't know that," Anna croons. I know she's only trying to comfort me. Adults pull this bullshit when they don't know how to explain what's happening. Mama's dying, and I know it.

"What are we going to do with the babies? Dad can't do this on his own. I can't do it. I'm only a kid."

Anna squeezes me harder. She's propping me up with faux confidence as she kisses the top of my head and says, "You'll be surprised what even a kid can do when there are no other choice. We'll cross that bridge when we get there. For now, we wait."

Hours pass before the doctor emerges from the double doors and asks us to join him in a private office. Dad tries to hold himself up to look respectable. Anna and I stand together behind his chair.

"I'm Dr. Hernandez, and I've been taking care of Mrs. Richards."

Fear crawls through my body and makes my hands and feet feel heavy. I blurt out what's on my mind, "Mama died."

All three of the adults in the room turn to look at me. They are shocked that I said it.

Dr. Hernandez takes a deep breath. "Just a minute, please," he says to me, and then looks down to my dad. "The babies are perfect. I've requested the NICU doctors to give them a once-over to be sure they didn't suffer any injuries from the prolonged delivery." He studies the folder in his hands. "Baby A was six pounds, three ounces, and Baby B was five pounds fourteen ounces. Both babies were nineteen-and-a-half inches long. They both gave me a good cry when we got them out, and I expect they are going to be fine."

Anna lets out a deep breath and puts her hand on her chest. "Thank God," she whispers.

It's great news about the babies, but I'm not relieved by knowing. "What about Mama?" I ask.

He shakes his head. "Mrs. Richards hasn't woken up. We sent her for a CT once we closed up the surgery. The radiologist gave me the report before I came to speak with you. Your mother has suffered a brain aneurysm. This kind of thing can happen. Either from the stress of the delivery, or sometimes, from a congenital weakness she's had since birth. It's more common than I'd like to say. We won't know how extensive the damage is until she wakes up. If she wakes up." He pauses. "I'm sorry."

I lean into Anna, who wraps her arm around my shoulders to hold me up. Anna whispers, "She's going to wake up and everything will be fine. She's in God's hands. Trust that he can do anything, and miracles can happen."

Her words infuriate me. I look to my Dad, waiting for him to say anything. He doesn't. Instead, he cries. He doesn't even ask when he can see the babies. He doesn't ask when he can see her.

11

If he wasn't always drunk and unreliable, this wouldn't have happened. If he could keep a job, Mama wouldn't have decided on a home birth to save money. This is his fault. All of this is his fault.

"Where is Mama? When can I see her?" I ask.

The doctor's face softens when he says, "Wait here. I'll go see if she's settled into her room yet."

~

When we're escorted into her room, Dad can hardly look at her. He sits in the chair beside her bed and takes her left hand. He kisses it tenderly as his tears spill on to her skin. The anger I feel for him is making me sick. *Why can't he find a way to be a man—the man we need him to be—and make this whole thing better?* I'm desperate for him to do something to make this better. Take charge. Tell me its fine. I could believe it if he said it. *Couldn't I?*

I sit on the other side of Mama's bed and start talking to her. "Mama, can you hear me? The babies are so great. They're healthy. You did it! You should wake up so you can see them. They need you. I need you." I repeat myself several times until the tears start to fall, and I continue repeating these words until the tears dry up again. My throat is raw, and I'm exhausted from my head to my toes. I keep begging her to wake up. I beg her not to leave me. I beg her to talk to me. When I finally give up, I look over and see Dad has fallen asleep in the chair. He's still holding her hand.

I'm not sure how much time has passed, and I'm disoriented as I look around the hospital room. Anna isn't here. I wonder where she could be then it occurs to me—she's probably with the babies. I've been so absorbed with Mama that I haven't even thought of going to see the twins. Mama was going to name them Brady and Brandon. I hope Dad doesn't change that. He's been less than involved since he knocked Mama up, so he really shouldn't get a say. The twinge of anger burns the back of my mind, but I'm too tired for any more emotions.

Anna's words echo in my mind, over and over again, *"It's going to be fine."* I want it to be fine. I need for Mama to wake up. I need her to come home, to take care of the babies, and to take care of me. Living without her isn't something I can process. My mind wanders in a hazy fog. Silently, I reprimand myself for being a selfish brat for thinking about my upcoming dances, graduations, awards banquets, driving, and having a real boyfriend. All things I need Mama to see me through.

I lie down in a small spot on the bed next to Mama's feet, careful not to jostle her. I remember Anna saying that all of this is in God's hands, so I close my eyes and start praying. Before I can finish listing everything, I need to ask God for, I'm asleep.

I wake up when I feel a squeeze on the fingers of my hand. It's a tiny feeling, light like a tickle. Slowly, I open my eyes and sit up. Mama's eyes are open, and her mouth is moving like she's trying to speak. She's holding my hand, and I scoot closer to get a better hold of her hand in return. She's still trying to speak, but I can't hear her—just a faint sound.

Leaning my ear down to her, I whisper, "Say it again, Mama."

Her voice is softer than before. "Take care of the babies. Take care of your daddy. I love you." She repeats it several times.

Hot tears start rolling down my cheek. "I will, Mama. I will. Stay with me." I press the nurse call button. "Stay with me, Mama," I beg.

Chapter 2

Now

When I dreamed of settling into a home of my own, and putting together a nursery, I never dreamed it would be under these circumstances. I thought it would be when I was happily married to my soulmate. We would have an amazing wedding. Small and intimate, but completely beautiful. I thought I would be barefoot on a grassy hill wearing a gauzy white dress. There would be flowers in my hair and tears threatening to spill down my cheeks. I would be holding the hands of my one, true love.

He would look at me with absolute adoration. I would return his gaze with teary eyes as we made promises to love and cherish through sickness and health, and all that. I would later tell him about the pregnancy, and he would weep with joy. I would cry with him as he fell to his knees and thanked God for such an amazing woman. He would wrap his arms around my waist, burying his face into my stomach, trying to communicate with our newly-formed baby. An act that would communicate his deepest love for both the baby and for me.

We would return from our month-long honeymoon on a tropical beach to shop for houses. We would buy a five-thousand-square-foot, three-story house in the best neighborhood. My husband is, of course, wealthy because he owns his own business. I don't have to work, so I set up our house and work on growing the perfect baby. When not decorating the perfect nursery, I brunch with my friends because ladies brunch together. I would, naturally, abstain from any alcohol, and beam with pride at the good choices I make for this little one. Life would be perfect.

Yeah, right. That's a fantasy land that only exists in dreams.

No, I'm doing everything backward.

I sit on the floor of the living room, taking in the house that was gifted to me. It's not very big. It's an ancient, two-bedroom house that Ryan and his *wife,* Rhae, remodeled themselves. The simple act of thinking his name fills my mind with all the things I miss about him, and that is everything. I'm still in love with him. He was what I had hoped my first relationship and eventual husband might be. My chest aches as I think of all the perfect things we could have been together.

I close my eyes and lay back on the floor as I recall the warmth on my skin, and the way the wind whipped my long blonde hair behind us as we rode around town in his Jeep—no top, no windows, no doors. It was absolutely terrifying and thrilling at the same time. We laughed so much my face hurt from the effort. By the end of the day, I couldn't smile from the pain in my face muscles, but I couldn't not smile either. The weather was stupid hot as it was nearing the end of June. If we observed every code orange warning, we would've never gone outside. But that's life in the Mid-South.

I was always wearing white shorts and a pink tank top with a pair of flip flops when we would go out. It's my summer uniform of sorts. Although, flip-flops aren't practical for riding around in a Jeep. They make it hell to get in and out of the damn thing. Still, I was happy any time I got to be with him. Our last ride together was tense for me. I knew something I needed to share with Ryan. It was torture not blurting it out as soon as I saw him, but I needed confirmation from the health department first.

That day was extremely special to me, but as usual, he left to go home to his wife at the end. His leaving was always a crushing blow to my ego. He wouldn't divorce her for me, and I had to accept what he was willing to give me. That's just the way it was. It always seemed like I was begging for his attention. He never had time to stay with me. I was such an idiot for thinking I would be enough to change his mind. He loved her. Really loved her.

I was stupid enough to think our love was stronger, and that I could *win* him from her. I'm a horrible person for ever having that affair. I should've left when he told me where I stood in the pecking order. Still, I stayed. I often wonder what would've happened if I'd been strong enough to stand up for what was right and walk away. I never had to figure out if I was strong enough to leave because Ryan died in a car accident.

The day he died, he called to break our plans because his wife needed him to help one of her sisters or something. I was irate and blurted out the secret I'd been saving. I told him I was pregnant in a mean and spiteful way. Something so monumental was reduced to a bratty tantrum. I would do anything to take back the words I spat at him. I should have waited until happier times. I should have told him on the last day we spent together. No matter what I should have done, I can't change what I did. I can't take the words back. He died without knowing how much I truly loved him and prayed that we could be together.

As Mama used to say, *"Control what you can control."*

I ponder her words and ask myself, "What can you control?" I can unpack this house, focus on getting settled, and plan for the delivery of this baby. Reaching down, I caress my growing belly, and remind myself that I can't regret my time with Ryan. I have this beautiful baby to think of now. He is going to look just like his dad with honey brown hair, and green eyes. I daydream that he might be an ace pitcher on the little league baseball team, or maybe a star quarterback. He's going to change the world. He's already changed my world and me.

I can see imperfections in the work Rhae and Ryan did on the house, but that's because I have an outsider's perspective, which is fitting for the situation. Things on the surface look amazing, but when the perspective changes it's easy to see the perfection is an illusion. Hindsight and all that. It occurs to me that they likely knew about the flaws but appreciated what they represented in the scheme of their life together.

I'm pulled from my thoughts when the front door opens, and I hear Mrs. Irma's voice. "Hello? Mel, baby, you here?"

I smile. "Yes, ma'am. I'm here," I call out as she's closing the door behind her.

"Where are ya, baby?"

I try to sit up, but can't. My awkward belly is heavy, and even rolling to the side, I can't seem to figure out how to get my feet under me. My efforts leave me breathless. "Stuck on the living room floor," I call out.

Mrs. Irma steps through the doorway from the kitchen to the living room. She stares for a moment, then asks, "Whatcha doing?"

I chuckle. "Well, I was having a rest, but now I'm stuck. I don't think I can get up."

"Baby, ya look like a turtle that got flipped on its back. I guess its good ya ain't in the middle of the road."

We both laugh. I'm wiping away tears when she says, "Let me see if I can help ya."

"Just give me your hand. I don't want you to get hurt helping me. You aren't strong enough to lift," I caution her.

Irma looks offended. "I'm stronger than I look."

I met Irma when Rhae gave me the house. She wanted me to have dinner with her family. Irma is the neighbor from down the street who treated Rhae like family. It's as if Irma knew the future and how Rhae would fit into her life. I've come to learn that Mrs. Irma knows a lot of things that don't make sense to the rest of us. After Ryan died, Rhae met Irma's grandson, Cade. He is part of the reason I have this house. Rhae moved to New Orleans with Cade to start a new life without the memories this house held for her.

Before that happened, Rhae and I had only met one time. When I got the news of Ryan's passing, I went to visit with her and tell her about the baby. She was irate in a calm way that made me think I pushed her over the line. In my experience, calm anger is much more deadly than the loud, aggressive kind. Rhae was completely justified in feeling that way toward me; I committed the ultimate betrayal. By the end of our visit, she said I was good people, and I left her with my number. I had gone to see her to have a way to connect my baby to his father, or his family. I honestly thought she hated me. I hated myself for a long time because of what happened. I thought wouldn't ever hear from her again.

It was a surprise when she found me at school one day and presented the idea of giving me the house. She said, *"Ryan can still provide for his child, even though he's gone."* When I glanced over the papers she handed me, I was in shock. My whole world came to a standstill as I read what she was doing. Who gives someone a freaking house? All I had to do was sign the papers. Of course, as with anything, she had a condition attached. *"You're going to need a support system to raise that baby. Come to dinner tonight. The address is on the papers. I want you to meet my family."*

Anna and Sunny, my somewhat adoptive parents, had offered to go with me, but this was something I had to do on my own. I was four, almost five months along when all of this happened. I was emotional and hormonal, but I wanted desperately to trust someone. At the time, I wasn't sure how much I should rely on Anna and Sunny to help with the baby. They are still raising my twin brothers. How much can I ask of them? I also didn't know how important the people at that dinner would become to me. It was a good decision.

I met all of Rhae's family including Mrs. Irma. Irma being the greatest grandmother I could have asked for; for both the baby and me. She told me all kinds of stories about her marriage to Cade's grandfather, who passed shortly after Ryan did. Fifty years of marriage, three children, and countless grandchildren was the summary of an epic love. There's a pang of loneliness in my chest when I consider those old stories of love that last forever. *Will I ever have that?*

Irma and I have spent a good deal of time together since then. She tells me stories about her childhood. I find her to be a fascinating human and am more than impressed with the things she has experienced. The more time I spend with her, the more I think of that corny adage regarding the two dates on a headstone, but the most important part being that dash between the dates.

Corny, but true. So much happens in the dash. The dash being a sad summary that says, "I lived." There's no telling if Irma will ever get around to telling me all of her stories, but it is something I love about her, and I will always make time to hear from her.

"C'mon, baby," she says as she reaches for me.

I take the small hand she offers. The contact scares me because I'm worried I'll pull her over or hurt her tiny hand. She begins to tug, and I'm grateful for her strength as I'm off the floor quickly.

"Teamwork, sweetie," she says as she tries catching her breath.

"Yes, ma'am. I promise I won't lie down on the floor again. Did I hurt you?"

"Naw. I'm just old. How's that baby girl doing?" she asks.

I smile and give her a side-eye glare. "Mrs. Irma, you know I don't know the gender. I think the baby is a boy, though." I'm making a gentle attempt at correcting her assumption. Again. We've argued back and forth for a couple of months now. I don't have the money to pay for an ultrasound, so I can't settle this definitively until I give birth.

She smiles her knowing smile, reaches out to rub my belly, and says, "*She* is going to be as beautiful as her mama."

And that's that. Irma will not be swayed. Rhae and Cade had both warned me that Mrs. Irma knows things. They never elaborated on the subject other than to say I should always trust her. *"She's never been wrong since I met her,"* Rhae would say.

I've seen her read palms and tell people their fortunes. It always seems like a parlor trick. But everybody in the south knows a little old lady who's bossy, aggressive, and mysterious. It's another southern quirk. Like old ladies read fortunes—totally normal. She's never offered to read me, so I don't make a big deal about it.

"Mel, what do you want to do with these boxes?" Irma's voice pulls me out of my thoughts.

"Oh, don't move that one. It's super heavy. I'll get the twins or Sunny over here to move it."

She laughs. "The twins are how old again?"

I smile thinking of my little brothers, Brady and Brandon. "They're eleven."

She smiles. "I do enjoy those boys. What about your dad? Is he coming to help, too?"

I shrug. "You know things with Daddy aren't..." I trail off without finishing. Dad and I still aren't on great terms, and I don't know that we ever will be. It makes me sad to think of him or talk about how he's doing. Frankly, it's depressing because I never have anything good to report about him.

Irma nods. "I know, baby. Well, I'm going to pick a mess of greens and get them started. Come down and get some later,

23

okay?"

"Yes, ma'am. Do you have purple hull peas in the freezer?"

She feigns offense. "What kind of operation ya think I'm running over there? Invite the boys to Sunday dinner this week. I'll make some cornbread."

I squeeze her into a tight hug and say, "Thank you," in her ear. She squeezes me back.

Later, when Brady and Brandon show up with Sunny, I start calling out orders like a drill sergeant. I tried to label the boxes for the rooms they belonged in, but those boys don't read. They grumble about how mean I am, and Sunny gets them back in line quickly. Anna and Sunny started acting like our parents after my mama died.

Anna is a petite woman with dark hair streaked with white and gray. Her eyes are a grayish blue, and she's as no nonsense as Mrs. Irma. They get along famously. Primarily, I think their friendship is tied to the fact that they are practically the same person—thirty years removed.

Sunny, on the other hand, is a tall, rotund, outspoken, gruff biker. He has the stereotypical beard, and a gas-mixed-with-cigarettes aroma. The most important things in this world for Sunny are Anna, his bike, and his bar. He is Anna's direct opposite. Sunny would do anything for his Anna, and jumps through whatever hoops she sets for him. They essentially raised us after Mama died because Daddy is a damn drunk and proved to be completely useless.

Sunny came to visit after Mama's funeral. He asked me to go to my room because he needed to talk to my dad. I did as I was told, but listened from my door. Sunny told my dad that he needed to get his shit together and clean up his act. He reminded my dad that there were now three children depending on him, and the drunk act wasn't going to cut it anymore. I still kind of laugh to myself when I remember Sunny telling him to *"man the fuck up."*

Dad didn't do any of that. I guess we didn't matter enough for him to get better.

Sunny and Anna took us to live with them that day. We never moved back home with my dad. He gets to visit with us when he's sober, but Anna still refuses to let the twins be alone with him for longer than a couple of hours.

As with so many other things in life, it's a constant struggle for Daddy. He makes six months being clean, and then relapses. I think this current sobriety run is approaching eight months. I keep hoping that this will be the final attempt. All the TV shows about addiction remind me that my hopes are probably in vain.

My family is all kinds of screwy. I learned at an early age that family isn't always about blood. Sometimes, it's about people who are there and supportive because blood relations don't rise to the occasion. In this way, I'm surrounded by the best people I could pick. For this, for my baby, I'm thankful. He will have a family life I could only imagine.

MEG FARRELL

Chapter 3

Acquaintances

I'm not sure if it's the pregnancy or moving that has me so exhausted. All I know, for sure, is this is going to be an extremely long night at work. I can't stop yawning. All I really want is to crawl in bed and stay there for a few days. Still, the bills won't pay themselves, so to work I must go. No one said I have to do it cheerfully, though.

I've been trying to think ahead and save up for the hospital bills that will come when the baby is born. It's almost a mantra as I keep reminding myself why I'm doing what I do. As the thought crosses my mind, he kicks and flips over. I rub my belly and say, "Shhhh, baby boy. You are worth everything I'm going through to get you here. We'll nap together when this over." I hope I'm right about that. People are always offering up their sleep-deprived horror stories, and I try to ignore them for the most part. Somehow, I know they are all true, but it's not as if I can turn back because I might miss out on some sleep. All these stories do is frustrate me.

My drive to work is nothing remarkable, and I arrive early to help Sunny get the bar stocked. The February air is still freaking cold. I shiver as I knock on the locked door and wait for Sunny to let me inside. He's probably in the office working on the liquor order and pissy about the bookkeeping. I was excellent at math in school, and I was thinking of becoming an accountant. I do what I can to make the numbers game a little bit easier for old Sun. I was in college to be an accountant when I met Ryan and got pregnant. School is on hold until after the baby is born, though. It's the best thing to do. That way I don't miss too much class, or have to drop any classes when I'm on maternity leave.

Sunny finally makes it to the door. "Hey, girl. Sorry it took me so long to hear you. You ain't frozen, are you?"

I shake my head. "Nope, but almost. What are you up to?"

He locks the door behind me as he answers, "Monthly liquor order and trying to do the books."

We both groan, which makes me laugh. "Hey, have you thought about how maternity leave will work with us not having insurance and benefits?"

Sunny looks at me over the rim of his glasses. "Nope. I figure we'll handle everything as we always have—as it happens. Why plan ahead?"

I smile. "Right. Need any help, old man?"

"Hey, now. That's not funny. I'm not old. I'm forty-five with many years of experience."

"Whatever, old man. Want me to take those tills out to the registers?"

"Yeah. Then do an inventory of the well bottles. I think Chastity was giving away drinks last night. Can I ask a favor?" He looks slightly more grumpy than usual.

"Anything."

"Watch her tonight. I will fire her ass so fast."

"You got it."

Admittedly, it's got to be weird for the customers of Dancin' Cowboys to have a pregnant bartender. The community we're in isn't necessarily wealthy. So I'm sure they all understand that a job is a job and babies ain't cheap. Pregnant or not, I have to work. I go to the register and put the till in, then pull up the inventory application. I print off the latest reports and start counting bottles in the inventory room, comparing them to the report. Sunny was right. We're short on vodka and whiskey. Curiosity gets me, and I repeat the process to inventory the top shelf bottles. We're short there, too. I give Sunny the information he needs.

"Thanks, hon. I knew it. I'm not even letting her work her shift tonight. I'll be completely broke at this rate."

Sunny fires her before she has a chance to clock-in. She

makes a hell of a scene but leaves before he needs to call the police.

Sunny says, "Sorry about having to fire her. Are you going to be okay on the bar alone tonight?"

I nod. "Of course! Piece of cake."

"I'm calling in some reinforcements because I know how stupid Saturday night can be. We're going to need someone to cover the floor. No promises, but I'll try to get some help in here."

"What's the worst that can happen? Bubba has to wait a little longer for his Jack and Coke? It won't be the end of the world, or the end of your bar. We'll be fine," I reassure him.

"Thanks for looking out for me, kid," he says as he wraps me in a big hug. It doesn't last but a second because he jumps back. "Woah! What the hell?"

I laugh and rub my belly. "That was the baby saying he loves you, too."

Sunny smiles. "That baby is strong! Still thinking boy?"

"Yeah. He's been kicking more lately."

Still smiling, Sunny asks, "How much longer?"

I think for a minute, doing math in my head. "Six weeks, or so. I think."

He smiles. "That's soon! Are you ready?"

I hesitate but try to be reassuring. "I still have to put the

30

nursery together. I've been collecting a few things here and there with my tip money. Still got a lot to do, though. I want to paint, and…"

"No, goofy. Are you ready to deliver that baby? I don't give a shit about a nursery."

"Oh!" I laugh at his directness. "Yeah. I mean I worry about what happened with Mama. Like, will that happen to me? But I've come this far, I have to see it through now." I take a seat on one of the bar stools. What I don't tell him is how scared I am. I've gotten pretty good at keeping emotions from showing on my face. It's been a necessity to get through this pregnancy. It's absolutely terrifying to remember Mama dying after the boys were born. I have no idea what would happen to my baby if I have a stroke during the delivery. There's no way Anna and Sunny could start over raising a new baby. They could; it just wouldn't be fair.

Sunny takes a seat on the stool next to me. His face is serious when he asks, "What does the doctor say?"

I shrug and look down. I'm swinging my feet, but I can't see them. All I see is belly. Thinking about what to say and not coming up with anything great, I sit quietly.

Sunny tugs at my chin to make me look at him. "What does the doctor say? Did you tell him about what happened with your mom?"

I nod. "I told him. Dr. Peterson says that it's completely different now. That was over ten years ago. And that knowing

Mama had a stroke gives us some information about what to watch for. He gave me a blood pressure cuff thing to use at home. I check my blood pressure a couple times through the day."

"And?"

"So far, it's good." Everything's been perfectly fine the entire pregnancy. I don't tell him how I worry that, at some point, things won't be okay. Sunny doesn't need to know how I don't sleep for being anxious about the birth and that what happened to my mother will happen to me.

Sunny sighs and seems relieved. "Alrighty, kid. You'll let us know if anything changes?"

"I will," I reassure him, but my heart's not in it.

~

It feels like everyone in town is at the bar tonight. If it's not a record number of customers, it's the fact that reinforcements haven't arrived, making it seem like a ton more people than usual. I'm slinging drinks like a mad woman. Wait times are up for mixed drinks, so I make two of everything ordered. This helps me stay a little bit ahead. It's not much help, really. Customers that know me and Sunny are patient and do a little bit of crowd control. I'm thankful for our regulars because they are awesome. They tip well and are willing to wait for a drink. Although, snapping the caps off of beers is quick.

The baby belly gets in the way a little bit, but only in terms of my being swift on my feet. If I can stand in one spot or only take one step, it helps make life easier for me. Still, I have enough experience tending bar to make the night work. Sunny helps as a bar-back since I can't lift cases of anything. He's been hauling ice all night and keeping the beer cooler stocked for me. We make a pretty great team; although, he complains all night. Mostly, it's swearing about having to fire Chastity. I feel bad when I notice how sweaty he gets. Still, he's a hard worker and won't let me suffer through it alone.

At the end of the night, I walk the last of our customers out and lock the door, then turn to lean my back against it. It feels good to just rest for a few minutes. There's no telling how much longer I'll be able to work a full shift standing on my feet. Exhausted doesn't begin to cover the feeling creeping through my body. Even the baby is tired. He stopped flipping about half way through my shift.

I look around the bar, and it is a hot mess. Without any backup tonight, no one was cleaning. There are bottles piled everywhere, full ashtrays, and bits of food that got dropped and never picked up. It's pretty gross. Pushing off the door, I start making a mental list of everything I need from the broom closet to get this mess under control. I grab a push broom, the mop, a bucket, pine cleaner, a bottle of sanitizer, some clean cloths, and rubber gloves. I tug a large garbage bag out of the box nearest the door on my way out of the closet.

I set all the cleaning supplies down on the bar, put the gloves on, and start picking up trash. When I'm mid-way through the room, Sunny drops bottles into the bag and takes it from me.

No words are exchanged. It's his place, and he's going to help out. What's there to talk about? We work in silence until Sunny goes over to the jukebox and starts some classic rock music. He's nothing if not consistently predictable. I love him, and the thought makes my heart swell.

After we get all the garbage picked up, he sweeps and I mop. As we're admiring the work we've completed, Sunny groans. "Did you check the bathrooms?" he asks.

My shoulders slump. "Nope. Forgot. I'll go do it now."

Sunny nods. "I'll be in the office. Let me know if you need help in there."

I walk toward the back hallway. The men's room stinks, but is otherwise not bad. I decide to tell Sunny what needs to be done in there and he can do it at his leisure. I can't stand that smell long enough to eradicate it. I'd end up sick all over the place, which would make more work for Sunny.

Next, I step into the ladies' room. I'm walking into each stall to check the toilets and the small trash cans. I've gotten two bags combined into one, and I step into the last stall. I squeal and jump back, letting the door slam shut. *What the fuck?* My heart has relocated to my throat as I process what I just saw in that stall. Slowly, stepping forward, I gently push the door open again.

There's a man curled up in the floor of the stall. He seems to be tall, judging by how his legs are folded under him. He's wearing jeans and a light blue, checked cowboy shirt, which look good with his tan skin and blond hair. I'm studying him, trying to see if he's breathing. I can't tell, so I squat down and hold the back of my hand up to his nose. There's not a strong flow of air against my hand, so I pinch his nose closed. When I've held it closed for a couple of seconds, his mouth pops open and he shifts away from my hand, swatting at me.

I laugh and immediately cover my mouth so I don't wake him up. I realize, too late, that not waking him is silly. That is exactly what I should be doing. I'm about to go fetch Sunny to kick him out when his phone starts to ring. It startles me, but maybe this could be a good thing. Whoever is calling can come get him. It'll save Sunny a call to the police department if someone can come help.

The sound is muffled, and I realize the phone must be in one of his pockets. It's likely in the pocket on the side that's sitting on the floor. I tug at his shoulder, trying to get him to move. There's no way I can move him fully, but I'm trying to get him to shift about an inch so I can get to the cell phone. At first, my efforts are wasted, and the phone stops ringing. *Hell!* I try again to get him to move. This time he shifts a tiny bit. The only problem is that he flops over on the floor, smashing his face and letting out a painful moan. I'm grimacing and worrying about whether or not I hurt him when his cell starts ringing again. It's a country song that seems familiar, but I'm not sure I can name it.

I start trying to slide my hand into his pocket again. This time I'm successful at fishing the phone out, but not before the damn thing stops ringing again. It's my turn to groan. I take an ungraceful seat on the toilet in the stall and shove him with my foot. I really couldn't give a shit about waking him up. I mean, the face smashing move to the floor didn't wake him up.

Moving this guy took a lot of what little energy I had left, and I need a minute to catch my breath. I'm beginning to think we'll have to call the police after all. It takes almost five minutes for the phone to ring again. When it does, I answer quickly.

"Hello?"

The caller is hesitant when he says, "Um, hi. Who is this?"

I smile a little bit, thinking about how fun it would be to mess with the guy on the floor and whoever this is on the phone. It would be easy to pull some shit on them. Ultimately, I decide I'm too tired to mess with a prank. "I'm Melody. I work at Dancin' Cowboys. I was cleaning the ladies' room and found this guy curled up in a stall."

He laughs and I can't help but smile in response. It's a comforting sound. "Nice to meet you, Melody. I'm Clayton. That guy would be Trey. He's known for drinking too much and then curling up on tile floors in front of toilets. The ladies' room, huh?"

I chuckle. Whoever this person is knows his friend pretty well. "Yep. He's pretty shitty. I managed to get him flopped over to get the ringing phone out of his pocket, but I don't think I can manage to get him off the floor."

"Understandable. I can come get him."

"Great."

"I'm, uh, kind of new in town, though. Can you tell me how to get there?"

"Sure thing." I give him directions and hang up, then walk out to the bar area. Sunny is leaning on the counter, waiting for me.

"Everything okay in there?"

I shake my head. "Nope. Drunk guy passed out. Sleeping in the ladies' room floor. Guess we should've checked the bathrooms before locking up." I raise my eyebrows in a gesture that suggests we should've known better.

Sunny nods. "Do I need to call the cops?"

I hold up the cell phone and place it on the bar. "Nah. His cell was ringing. It was a guy looking for him. He's on his way to collect his friend."

Sunny grumbles. "We should have called the police. I'm going to wrap up in the office while you wait for this guy. Don't open the door without me."

"I didn't get to finish the men's room. You might need to get to that first."

Sunny rolls his eyes and changes course toward the men's room instead of the office.

Fifteen minutes later, there's a knock at the front door. Sunny comes out of the hallway right before I start turning the deadbolt. He must have his handgun on him because he reaches around to his hip before nodding, telling me it's okay to open the door. When he does, I call, "Who is it?"

"Clayton. We spoke on the phone. I'm here for the drunk."

I chuckle, unlock the door, and then step aside to let him squeeze through. When he's inside, I lock it again. Sunny stands back and gives Clayton the signature *dude* nod. It's neither polite nor aggressive. A gesture that says, *"Handle ya business and go."*

Clayton returns the *dude* nod, looks back at me and asks, "So, ladies' room?"

I laugh because of the testosterone and tension in the room. "Yeah, this way," I say and escort him to the ladies' bathroom. "Here ya go. Your buddy is in the last stall."

He smiles and I melt. I mentally chastise myself. There is no way I need to have these thoughts about anyone right now.

"Thank you for letting me come get him instead of calling the police."

I return his smile. "Of course. Are you in the habit of rescuing this guy?"

"You could say that," he answers and turns up the wattage on his smile.

"You might want to think about either getting him in rehab or assigning someone to watch him when he goes out. He doesn't seem like a good friend if you have to do this a lot."

"I would agree with you, except, he's not my friend. He's my brother."

"Brother?"

He nods. "Yep. Kid keeps me on my toes. He really shouldn't drink unsupervised. Do you know if he had anybody with him tonight?"

I shake my head. "Sorry. I was tending bar by myself. I didn't really get to pay attention to much of anything. I was trying to keep my head above water, if you know what I mean."

As we're standing in the doorway talking, I can't help but take in his height. He's really freaking tall. I'm not very tall myself, but this is no perception thing. I could swear he's over six feet tall. I consider how much they look alike in a true comparison. It's hard to tell right now because one's face is flat on the floor while the other has a thick, dark beard covering most of his face. There's definitely a difference in the color of their hair. Clayton's hair is dark brown like his beard, and it is strikingly different from his brothers. Are Trey's eyes the same intense dark brown as Clayton's?

They definitely have the same bubba-swag, cowboy style. Clayton is also wearing a checked, button-down cowboy shirt. However, he has his tied around his waist. He's also wearing a white T-shirt and blue jeans. The shirt looks dirty, and his jeans are more than a couple years old by the wear in the knees. I start to wonder if he plays sports, because I can tell how leanly muscular his body is under the T-shirt.

"Hello?" he says.

I blink once, clearing my head of all the places my thoughts want to go with that body. "Yes?" I ask.

"You must be exhausted. You totally checked out for a second there. Thanks for staying. I'll get him out of here, now."

Before I can say anything else, he walks to the stall, bends down and lifts his brother to his feet. Trey comes around enough to see his brother has got him. He mumbles, "Hey, Clay." His words are slurring, and I'm sure the smell rolling off him is noxious. I shudder, thinking about all the times I had to help my dad when he was in a similar state. I don't envy Clayton right now. But the fact that he calls his brother Clay is so sweet. He sounds like a child.

Clayton is kind as he says, "Hey, bud. Let's go home."

Trey manages a nod and makes an attempt to move his feet, which is actually less helpful than he thinks. But they start making their way to the front door.

Clayton laughs as his brother continues drunk mumbling, and I follow them. Sunny is there and helps get the doors for Clayton to take his brother to the car. I watch from the bar as Sunny talks to Clayton for a few minutes before they shake hands, and Sunny comes back inside.

"Go home, Mel. Get that baby some sleep," he orders.

"What did you tell him?"

"That he needs to keep a closer eye on his brother. And that if this happens again, I will call the cops."

"Sunny. You know you don't like calling the cops. You wouldn't let his brother come get him again?"

Sunny laughs. "You know I would. We actually exchanged numbers. I'll watch out for the kid when his brother can't be here. I don't know why, but I kind of like that Clayton guy."

I smile. "You're a big softy, Sunny! Just admit it." I'm sure it's just hormones and being near a nice looking, kind guy, but I like him too.

MEG FARRELL

Chapter 4

Check the Box

It's nearly noon when I wake up on Sunday. This pregnancy is getting old. I know I'm supposed to bask in every beautiful moment, but nothing about this experience feels beautiful anymore. The wonderment of all the changes my body went through and feeling the first kicks has gone. Now, I feel like I'm the size of a house. Slap a wide load banner on my ass and get out of the way. I'm always exhausted, hungry, emotional, or angry. Nothing fits, not even maternity clothes. I've been thinking I need to buy one of those old, southern-lady house dresses. I think they're called muumuus. It should have a huge floral pattern. I'm not wearing underwear or a bra. Saggy, sloppy, and comfortable. That's all I want right now—some kind of way to feel comfortable. Maybe I'll even get some orthopedic house shoes to go with it.

The only time I leave my bed is to go pee or make some food. That seems to be all I do anymore—eat, pee, and grow a baby. I do still work at the bar most nights, but when I can, I'm in bed. Sunny and Anna come by to drop off some baby clothes and toys they found at a resale shop. Since I can't afford the ultrasound to tell us the gender, everyone has been buying gender-neutral clothes. I dislike having so much green and yellow, but I can't seem to convince everyone it's a boy. Irma, on the other hand, buys dresses and hair bows. She's been knitting a pink baby afghan, too. She's hell-bent on this baby being a girl. I smile to myself. *She's going to be so upset when this baby gets here*.

Old and a little frailer each day, Irma can still fuss with the best of them. I try to be a believer in Irma's knowledge, but I can't bring myself to think the baby is a girl. I love Irma, so I don't challenge her too often. In another few weeks, the question will have an unequivocal answer. And no one will argue with either of us.

Sometimes, I try to imagine what having a baby will be like. Not raising or caring for a tiny, new life, but the actual mechanics. *Will it hurt? Will I be able to push him out? What if I have to have a C-section*? All the questions I have scare me to death. And this line of thought always brings me around to the memories of my mama. I worry about having a delivery as risky as Mama had with the boys. The home delivery she planned was meant to save the family money, and we didn't have insurance. At the time, I didn't know what that meant or how important it would be. Now that I'm faced with the huge hospital bills to pay for my own delivery with no insurance, I can sort of see the appeal.

Dad hasn't been able to hold down a steady job since I've

been alive. I don't know what made him drink the way he does, but Mama did all she could to compensate for it. She always tried to work, or when she couldn't, we would sell vegetables we grew in the backyard. We did anything and everything to make ends meet. I always had clothes people gave us, or she bought at the thrift store. My shoes always had holes or were ill-fitting. My friends at school would talk about their new cell phones, or their video games, and I wanted shoes that fit. I didn't know what it was like to have a nice pair of shoes that were only ever worn on my feet until we went to live with Anna and Sunny.

We were dirt poor. It was embarrassing when the church would put us on their Christmas benevolence list. They would bring us Christmas gifts and boxes of food so we could have Christmas dinner. I resented them because invariably some girl I envied at school would be with the group of people dropping the stuff off.

All of the struggles I watched Mama go through made me resent Dad even more. I rarely saw him get out of that chair other than to chase down another bottle of whiskey. Thinking back on it as an adult, I wonder when Mama got pregnant. *Wouldn't that require effort on Dad's part*? The thought sends a shudder through me. No one needs to think about their parents having sex.

Sunday evening, I decide to walk down to Irma's and help her can some of her garden veggies. We usually watch the singing talent shows together. Irma loves to hate those shows. It's the only reason she watches them.

"Woo!" Irma says dramatically, unimpressed when a particularly bad candidate sings.

"I know," I groan.

"Who told that baby she could sing? Someone should be honest with her, ya know?"

I laugh. "Then they wouldn't have a show. What would you do then?"

Irma grins. "I know. I do love it when they sound like a cat in heat."

We continue making fun of the ones who clearly have no place on the show and laugh at the dramatic prepared video that shows why winning would mean the world to the more talented ones. I often think about if I have what it takes to win or if some old lady would sit and make fun of my yowling.

I do believe Mrs. Irma has a thing for one of the celebrity judges. I don't dare say it because she would be offended at the idea that any man could hold a candle to her late husband. Our time on Sundays is a companionable time we both need. We're both alone in so many ways, yet we have each other. There's something to the rhythm of life we share. It's not something I can explain; just something I feel. She's precious to me. I shudder to think what would happen to me without her.

Sometimes, when the mood strikes, she asks me to sing for her. I know she prefers the old hymns, so sometimes I oblige her. Tonight is one of those occasions.

"Mel, baby, sing for an old lady. Please," she asks sweetly.

I smile. "Mrs. Irma, have I ever told you I used to want to be a singer/songwriter?"

She nods. "You didn't have to tell me. I already knew. Why else would yo' Mama name you Melody?"

I never thought about it until now. "That is an excellent point."

"Why, she could have named you Harmony, but then you wouldn't be a singer, would you? I imagine someone named Harmony playing accompaniment."

I gasp. "Mrs. Irma! You don't know that. Someone named Harmony could be a singer."

She waves her hands at me. "Pssshhh! Chile, I know what I know. Anyway, she could have named you any common name, but she picked Melody. Why do you think that is? Surely you have some idea."

I start to think what she could possibly be getting at, and frown because I keep coming up with nothing. Clearly, she has a point she's trying to make. "I give up," I finally announce.

She turns to face me, takes my hand and says, "Because, my love, you are a songbird. You are meant to be heard, to bring joy, and to connect people."

My smile is timid, but I can't just accept her rationale. I sigh, "Thank you, Mrs. Irma. I never asked Mama why she named me Melody, and it never came up on her end. She did love to hear me sing, and I loved to hear her voice, too. There's no way she could have known I would be a singer, though." As I'm answering Mrs. Irma, I'm trying to remember the sound of her voice as she would clean house on Sunday mornings, but it's not there. I can't remember what she sounded like. Has it been so long? Time has robbed me of that memory.

Interrupting my quiet panic, Mrs. Irma says, "Trust me on this. You should sing more."

I shrug and turn from her. "I don't know. It's like when I lost Mama. I didn't hear the music in my head anymore."

She's turned back to the TV and is rocking ever so slightly with her eyes closed. Finally, she says, "You'll sing again. Your dreams will return. Give it time, love."

Truth is, I gave up my dreams when I took on raising my brothers. I remember the fear of losing them or being put up for adoption because of my Dad's problems. It was a fear that kept me awake at night and made me even more driven to keep everything together so that it couldn't happen. I know that's why Sunny and Anna helped as much as they did. I couldn't let Mama down by losing the boys. Anna and I talked about it often. She was desperate to adopt the boys and raise us all. My persistent insistence that I could do it created a cautious situation where Anna and Sunny watched us like hawks—ever vigilant that I not fail.

Anna taught me about the babies and everything from

diapering to watching them for fever. She was there when I woke up in the mornings, and she stayed until the babies went down for the night. Every Saturday she taught me how to keep house. Sunny would come with her and play with the babies while we worked. By Saturday afternoon, she took me to the grocery store and helped me make meal plans for Dad and me. Once, she even took Dad to file for welfare and assistance so we could get diapers and other basics. Sunny did what he could with the handy work around the house. I learned what I could, but he still won't let me do the work on my own. Still. Sometimes his hovering is frustrating.

I miss the rest of the TV show thinking about everything that I can't change or fix. Worrying for no reason, because that's what I do. Irma and I have some dinner, and she packs some veggies for me to take home and cook later in the week. I squeeze her neck and tell her goodnight. Then I snuggle into my coat. Before I turn to leave, Irma insists I call her when I get home. I do so as she asks as soon as I get in the door.

Placing the veggies in the fridge, I decide what day I'll have the boys over for lunch one day before work. I walk into the room that will be the nursery and stare at the paint chips I have taped to the wall. For some reason, I just can't settle on a paint color, and it's making me restless. I need to decide soon so I can put the twins to work.

I promised them a sleepover in the new house before the baby comes. They were so excited that they offered to do anything to help me get the house ready for the baby. I hope they are willing to paint. Surely, they can manage it with Sunny's supervision. I'm thankful for the boys. I know they are turning out to be great men because of Sunny. God knows it isn't because of our Dad. *Stop it*, I reprimand myself. *He's sick. He can't help it.* I resent him, yet I can't help but make excuses for him. It's a miserable existence being the child of an addict of any kind.

I learned that I have great company in my misery when I attended group therapy at Anna's insistence. After a couple of years of that, I quit going. They weren't covering any new ground, and my guilt at the resentment I harbor for Dad was building up on me. I never did decide if therapy didn't work because of me or because of them.

I'm tired of staring at the paint chips and thinking about life. This is not getting me closer to deciding on a color. Frustrated, I start doing eeny-meeney-miney-moe to finalize my decision. It's a reasonable methodology; as reasonable as any other way. When I finish the rhyme for the third time, I'm pointing at a pale gray color. I shrug. "Could be worse," I say aloud. "At least other gender-specific colors will match it." The baby agrees by pressing his feet into my ribs, which causes me to lose my breath for a moment.

"Running out of room in there?" I ask him, rubbing my side.

He answers with another nudge.

Satisfied that I've finally made a decision, I take down the paint chips, circle the color I've chosen, and walk back to the living room to put the chip in my purse. I'll go to the store tomorrow to buy what I'll need to keep the boys busy. Sundays and Mondays are my only days off from the bar and I must start checking things off the growing pre-birth checklist.

~

The next morning, I'm up way before I intend to be. I've reached the stage of this pregnancy where I just can't sleep more than a little at a time. It's either heartburn, restless legs, or pain in my sides or back keeping me awake. *I'm so over this.* After some breakfast and a shower, I kick off my errand day by taking my old, beat up car in for an oil change. Sunny told me the damn thing will run forever if I will do simple maintenance to keep it healthy.

Normally, I would change the oil myself; however, there isn't a jack in this world tall enough to make room under ole Bessie for the belly and me. Even if I did get down under the car to change the filter, I wouldn't ever be able to get myself out. I know Sunny would do this for me in a heartbeat, but I need to be an adult and start doing for myself. I saw a coupon in the free, county newspaper for an oil change at Mr. Busby's Auto Repair. Should be an easy service. I reason that this shouldn't take more than thirty to forty-five minutes. I dig in my purse and locate the coupon prior to locking the front door and carefully navigating the steps down the front porch.

I drive to the shop as soon as it opens at nine a.m. The door covering the service bay starts rolling up as I pull into the parking lot. There's a familiar face standing in the middle of the bay, directing me. When I'm successfully inside, he motions for me to stop. I put the car in park and turn off the ignition. My door opens as I reach for my purse. As I turn to get out of the car, I look up into Clayton's smiling face.

"Well, Ms. Melody. What can I do for you today?"

God. He sounds like Rhett Butler from *Gone with the Wind.* I can't help but chuckle a little awkwardly. "Uh, how about you call me Melody. The Ms. is a bit strange. We're probably the same age."

His smile broadens. "Sorry. My mama raised me to be a gentleman, and I do my best to make her proud."

"Well, I'm not your grandmother." I return his smile. I'm careful with my sarcasm these days because I've been accused of being mean since I've been pregnant. It's all anyone seems to notice when I think I'm being funny. I can't be sure if I'm hormonal, mean, or sarcastic, I've been laying off.

His grin broadens and then he seems to rethink it. Sobering, he nods, "Noted. Melody. What can I do for you today?"

I reach into my purse, retrieve the coupon, and hand it to him. "This is for an oil change special. Buy three quarts, get the fourth quart free, and a free oil filter. This is all I want—no more, no less," I say. All business.

The broad smile stretches across his face again as he laughs. "Can do. Do you want to wait, or is someone picking you up?"

"I'll wait. The waiting room has heat, right?"

Clayton feigns offense as he pretends to clutch his non-existent pearls. "What kind of place do you think Mr. Busby is running? We aren't heathens."

I cut my eyes at him briefly. "Good to know. Lead the way."

Clayton escorts me to the waiting area. I take a seat as he goes behind the counter to ring me up. Mrs. Busby must do a lot to help her husband with the shop. The waiting area is clean and decorated with doilies and faux flower arrangements. The flowers have a bit of dust on them, though. There's a smell of potpourri in the air that blends with the odors of tires and oil. I know its Mrs. Busby's work. It seems as though she's trying to make it seem more comfortable in here for women. I could be wrong, but it doesn't seem like Mr. Busby or any of the mechanics would go to the effort. Too bad there's nothing she can do to hide the fact that it's still a repair shop.

I'm disappointed that the only magazines on the table are *Popular Mechanics*, *Car and Driver*, and some other racing magazine. I shake my head and think about why Mrs. Busby hasn't done more to diversify the reading materials. I reach into my purse for the paperback I've been reading for six months. I'm not much of a reader these days, but I keep something handy for such a situation. I'll finish it one day.

I'm starting to read when Clayton clears his throat. I look up. "Yes?"

"Would you like some water or a soda while you wait?"

I frown and think about it. I'm planning to stop at the hardware store after the shop. There's enough urgency to pee with this baby. "Uh, no. Thanks. How long will the car take?"

He smiles. "Less than an hour. I'll go get started."

Clayton has only been gone a few minutes, but I can't settle into this book. It's frustrating, and I realize that it's not my infrequent reading that is taking so long—I'm not into this book. Switching gears, I pull a small notebook from my purse. It's my songwriting book. I've kept a small notebook on hand since before Mama died.

Once I started playing guitar as a kid, I kept it because ideas were always popping into my head. Flipping it open, I turn to the last idea I started on in the back of the notebook. The date is depressing. It's been three years since I tried to work on this tune.

I spend a few minutes re-acquainting myself with the lyrics. A tune is dancing on the edge of my mind as I start to hum. Before, long I'm getting antsy because I can't seem to focus on anything. Shoving the notebook back into my purse, I walk over to the window and stare into the work area. There's an empty office chair near the computer system in the shop. Before I think about, I walk through the door and roll the chair over next to my car. Clayton is on the ground with his legs sticking out from underneath it.

I nudge his foot with the toe of my shoe as I sit down. "You know," I start. "I would be doing this myself if I could fit under the car right now."

His laugh is muffled. "Is that so?"

"It is. I learned from Sunny. He's always lecturing me about keeping this car running so I don't have to buy a new one."

"Is it killing you to bring it to a shop?"

I think about this for a second. "Yeah. It is. Plus, I can't sit in there alone. Are you the only person that works here?"

He laughs again. "Yeah. For today, I am. Mondays aren't huge on business. Doesn't make sense to have more than one mechanic on duty."

We sit in silence while he moves around the shop gathering materials and closing up the used oil pan. He's precise in his movements and keeps the shop tidy as he goes. His dark blue mechanic's Dickies are smudged with oil and grime. His height is still staggering to me, and I start to think about whether I've ever met someone as tall as Clayton. My eyes drift to his ass. I know I shouldn't be looking, but it turns out to be a very nice ass. I should be ashamed of myself for not being able to look away. My current reproductive status is the result of checking out nice asses. I really should learn from my mistakes.

I keep watching him as he reaches for an oil filter on the top shelf. His biceps are on full display, and my mouth goes dry. *What the hell, Melody?* He turns to resume work on my car, and our eyes lock. I snap my gaze away from his by staring at the floor, and then slowly look back up. He's smiling at me, and my face starts to heat. I know I'm blushing. I don't know what else to do, so I ask, "Where are you from?"

He chuckles and shakes his head as he starts pouring the new oil into the car. "Gulf Shores."

"What's so funny?" I ask. "Everything I say makes you chuckle at me."

"It's funny. You're funny. I catch you checking me out, and you're going to lead with the obvious, 'where are you from,' questions. Next, you'll ask, 'How long have you been here?' Answer: Six months yesterday. And, uh, close your mouth. You're going to catch flies."

I didn't realize my mouth had fallen open. I snap it shut, and then decide to correct his assumptions. "You're a real smartass. I wasn't going to ask that next. I was going to ask why you would move to Bell Hills. It's kind of nowhere."

He grins mischievously. "I am. And Bell Hills is not kind of nowhere. It *is* nowhere."

"Then why move here?"

He rolls a creeper over and takes a seat on it. Leaning forward with his elbows on his knees, he kind of looks like a little kid sitting on that thing. He wipes his hands on a dirty, blue handkerchief he's using as an oil rag. "Did you ever think that maybe nowhere is exactly where I want to be?" The smirk on his face is absolutely infuriating.

"Sorry. I was trying to make conversation."

He looks down at the filter, shaking his head, and says, "I'm sorry, too. Let's start over. Hi, I'm Clayton Murphy. You may remember me from the drunk-guy rescue mission Saturday night. I'm new in town. I moved up here six months ago from Gulf Shores, Alabama. What's your name?"

I smile, conceding to his little game. "I'm Melody Richards. I've lived in or around Bell Hills my entire life. I'm a Sagittarius, and thirty-four weeks pregnant. I take things a little too personally lately. Thanks for rescuing your brother the other night. I'm not sure in my current state I could have gotten him out of the bathroom."

Clayton holds out a dirty hand he tried to clean on the oil rag. "Nice to meet you, Melody."

I take his hand to shake it and warmth moves all over my body in a wave. My heart starts racing. I immediately try to look cool as I attempt to calm down from our interaction. There's something in the strength and callousness of his hand that makes me feel weak. I squeeze his hand harder as I shake it.

"Quite the grip, there," he says, laughing.

"God, I'm sorry," I say as I let go of his hand. I bet he can see the embarrassment crawling all over me. I'm certain my face is beet red.

He's laughing hard now. "No, no, it's fine." He gets up and starts wrapping up the work he's doing on my car. "Do you have major plans for the rest of your Monday?"

I give him a small smile. "Nope. Making a run to the hardware store and then heading back home."

"The hardware store, huh? What kind of project are you doing?"

I shrug. "I don't know if you would call it a project, necessarily. I need to paint the nursery for the baby." I rub my hand over my belly and the baby kicks in response.

He prints the invoice for the car, and instead of a price at the bottom, it says paid in full. Confused, I look at him, and he grins back at me.

"On the house. Pregnant lady special." He winks.

"Okay. Well, thank you, but I can pay." I've taken enough freebies out of necessity. I work for the money I need to take care of myself now. The last thing I want him to think is that I would use him for free services. I start digging in my purse for my wallet, and the paint chips tumble out onto the garage floor.

He stoops to pick them up and then says, "Looks like you have three shades of the same gray here."

Offended, I huff and snatch the chips back. "They are not the same. Typical man response. You can't see the subtle variations in these colors?"

"Woah, Melody. Maybe I didn't get a close enough look. Let me look again. Is the baby a boy or a girl?"

I frown and look away. Sighing, I say, "I don't know. I think it's a boy, but Mrs. Irma thinks girl."

"You didn't want to know the sex of the baby?" he asks a little perplexed.

I shake my head. "I can't afford the ultrasound to find out."

He nods, seeming to understand. "Well," he takes one paint chip from my hand. "This one has too much blue in it." He takes the two remaining chips and stares for a few minutes. "Go with this one." He hands one back to me.

I stare for a moment. "Why this one?"

He smiles. "It's lighter and has a more silver base. It's not plain gray. Plus, it's a good neutral. Anything you buy will match."

I'm staring at the paint chip and realize he's picked the one I picked last night. But he's also right; I *do* have three shades of the same gray. "You're saying all of that color blend nonsense because I have three shades of the same gray." I elbow him.

He takes the jab and laughs at me, then walks over to close the hood of the car. He starts checking the pressure of each tire. While he's adding air to the front driver's side tire, he says, "Make sure to tell your husband that Mr. Busby warranties all of our work. If anything happens after you leave here, give us a call and we'll come tow it for free. Then we'll give you a free diagnosis."

I roll my eyes, but he doesn't see. "I'm not married. But I'll keep that in mind." A wave of pissed-off energy rolls over me.

He looks up. "I'm sorry. Boyfriend, then?"

I shake my head. "Nope. I'm on my own. Doing it myself. Can I go now?"

"I'm sorry. I shouldn't make assumptions like that. It's just..."

I don't smile. "It's no big deal, really. Not everyone follows the traditional pattern, ya know?"

Clayton continues apologizing, but I wave it off.

"Please. Stop. A pregnancy doesn't mean I have a relationship with the baby's dad. I know that makes me a slut or whatever. I need to go." My anger is growing by the second. I'm not proud of the relationship that got me here, and it's not something I'm willing to talk about it. It's none of his business.

He hands me the keys as I take a seat in the car. "Look, I'm really sorry. I didn't know," he tries one last apology.

I take a deep breath. "I know you didn't. It's cool." I close the door, start the car and leave.

~

The whole way to the hardware store, all I can think is that he is a stupid-head boy that doesn't know any better, and I shouldn't be angry with him. But I am. The assumptions are worse than the situation. Should go around telling my business to every person I meet? Hell, I'm pregnant. That gives everyone in town the right to know how I got that way, doesn't it?

I'm still pissy and complaining to myself when I walk up to the paint counter. The older gentleman knows me pretty well since I moved into the house and have been coming in for advice. He's polite when he asks, "What can I do for you?"

I paste on a fake smile. "I need a gallon of this color in the eggshell finish." I slide the paint chip to him.

"Oh, good choice. What room are you painting?"

"It's going to be a nursery." I snap and gesture to my obvious physical state.

"Yes, ma'am," he says, looking a little taken aback by my answer. "Eggshell is a good choice for children's rooms. It's highly durable. I, uh, can have it ready in about thirty minutes."

I nod, feeling ashamed that I lashed out at him like I did. "Thank you, Jim. I'm going to have a seat over in the patio furniture area. Will you call over the intercom when it's ready?"

Jim shakes his head. "No, ma'am. I'll walk it over to you." He smiles, and I feel like a bigger pile of dog poo for snapping at him.

I walk to the patio furniture. I never understood why they

61

set up the furniture inside. It's going to be used outside, but I don't mind the chaise lounge I find to rest for a bit. I don't know why the assumption Clayton made is bothering me. He's only human. He did what everyone else in town has done—question my relationship with the baby's father. I haven't explained it to anyone other than family and close friends. No one wants to go around with a sign on that says, "Pregnant from an affair with a married man who died." *Why did I get angry with him so quickly?* These hormones have me acting like a maniac.

First, I'm staring at this guy's ass, and then I'm yelling at Jim over the paint. Mixing paint doesn't usually take long. I decide to try breathing exercises to calm down. I close my eyes and start counting my breaths in, holding for a few seconds, and breathing out. Around the fifth or sixth breath, I sigh and start to nod off.

I'm awakened when Jim gently nudges my shoulder. "Ms. Richards your paint is ready."

Slowly, I sit up and wipe the sleep from my eyes. "Oh! Thank you!" I try to get up, but I'm having some difficulty pushing off the chair. Jim has a small basket in his hands that he sets down beside me as he helps me to stand.

"This way, dear," he says as he picks up the basket and walks me to the register. "I took the liberty of pulling together some painting supplies. If you don't need something, just tell me, and I can go put it back."

"Thank you," I say as I start looking over the haul he's gathered. There's a two-inch angled brush, a roller set with tray and frame, a drop cloth, and some masking tape. There's nothing extraneous. "I'll take it all."

His smile is rewarding, and he proceeds to ring up my purchase. I'm slightly embarrassed to pay with tip money because it's a lot of ones. He doesn't seem to notice or care. When he finishes the transaction, he walks me to the car, and puts my things into the trunk. "Let me know if I can do anything else for you."

I smile and say, "Thank you, Mr. Jim. I'm sorry I spoke to you that way earlier."

"Nonsense, dear. I understand. Would you tell Irma I said, 'hello?'"

I nod quickly. "Sure will. Thanks again!"

I pull out of the parking lot, shaking my head. I won't tell Irma that Jim said 'hello.' She would lose her mind. Jim has had a thing for Irma for a long time, and she won't give him the time of day. It makes me wonder just how long he's had that flame burning. *Years*, I think.

MEG FARRELL

Chapter 5

Baby Shower

"Sunny!" I call out as I walk through the door for work and lock it behind me.

"Back here, doll," he answers.

Confused, I ask, "Back where? What are you doing?"

Sunny calls out again, "Here. In the office. Come help me."

I roll my eyes I slide off my jacket and put my purse on the bottom shelf of the rack behind the bar. I shake my head as I start for the office. When I reach the door, I notice the store room is decorated in pink, blue, green, and yellow. As I gaze around the gaudy room, it starts to slowly dawn on me what's happening. I step inside and a group behind me yells, "SURPRISE!"

I gasp and then cover my mouth to keep from squealing. Tears prick my eyes, and all I can say is, "Thank you." My voice is barely audible. Tears are making my throat thick. I swallow it back and try repeating myself.

Irma steps forward and pulls me into a hug. "We know ya need things for dis baby. Life has been hard, an' we want to make it better for ya, sweetness."

I squeeze her to me, and whisper, "Thank you so much."

Anna, my brothers, and Sunny take turns hugging me. Anna gets busy making cups of punch for some of the regular customers they invited to the shower. Next, she measures off pieces of crepe paper for some kind of game about the circumference of my belly. I frown but try to be a good sport.

Next Anna hands out safety pins, and Irma announces that everyone starts with a safety pin, but that if anyone says the word baby, they lose their pin. The person with the most pins at the end of the shower wins a prize. "I'm confident I'll be the winner," she says as a warning to the rest of the guests. Among the remaining guests are Rhae's sister and niece, as well as a couple of her friends. I think their names are Jules and Lucy. I met them the night Rhae had me over for dinner.

Rhae's sister, Jess, brings me a cup of punch. I hug her. "How've you been? I haven't see you in a while. Looks like Jillian has grown a foot in the last few months!"

Jess hugs me back. "I think she's having a growth spurt. She's either sleeping all the time or eating like her brother. You know, just shoveling food in her mouth as if she's starving to death. I worry about her weight, you know. Girls. It's so easy for us to pack it on and not realize it."

I smile and nod. "Yeah, but she's fine. Try not to worry about her. She'll level off. How's Connor and Coop?"

"Being men. Having man time. They're good if they're grubby and eating."

We both laugh.

"I, uh, didn't bring a gift," she stammers. "I thought I would see what all you get today at the shower, and then we can go shopping together some time."

I smile and take her hand. "That sounds perfect. Being that you have two kids, there are lots of things I want to ask you."

Jess looks a little confused. "Okay. Like what?"

"We'll talk more, but I'm worried about what delivering this baby will be like. The 'what if' questions are keeping me up at night."

She chuckles and gives me a knowing smile. "I got ya covered, kid. Now, give me that pin."

"Got me!" I laugh as I hand it over.

The shower is a sweet gesture, and after we all have a plate of appetizers that Irma and Jess made, they set me up to start opening gifts. At this point, Irma is winning the safety pin game. She's covered in them. She's not methodical about where she pins them on her shirt when she snags one. It's pretty funny, and I am thoroughly entertained.

When I take the first gift bag in hand, and start to pull it up, there's a commotion near the entry to the storage room.

"Are we late?" I look up to see Rhae and Cade walking so fast they're almost running.

Irma's face cracks open into a wide grin. "Of course you are! That grandson of mine drives slower than anyone I know!"

Cade crosses the room and scoops his grandmother up into a bear of a hug. "Sorry, Granny. I didn't mean to be late."

Irma starts swatting at his arms. "You put me down. This ain't dignified. At all!"

Laughing, Cade sets her on her feet and steps out of the way for Rhae to hug her. Rhae pats her sister's shoulder and comes over to hug me. "Hey, honey. How are you?"

I'm stunned, so it takes me a moment to reply, "I didn't expect you to be here."

Her smile is kind. "I know. I needed to be here for you. Here, open my gift first."

I do as she asks, and I pull out a pageant-quality white dress. The bag stills feels heavy, and I look down in the bottom. There's tiny patent white shoes, and a gift card to a department store. I shake my head. Irma must've told them her girl theory.

"Uhm, Rhae, I don't know the gender of the baby."

She laughs. "Irma says girl. I'm going with girl."

I chuckle. "Clearly. But what if it's a boy? You've bought this amazing dress. I'd have to return it."

Her smile is cocky. "Too bad I didn't save the receipt. What did I tell you about listening to Irma?"

I can't help but laughing. Irma is a mastermind. It becomes less shocking the more gifts I open. They are all girl clothes, gift cards, diapers, wipes, and little accessories I'll need to care for the baby. By the end of the pile of gifts, my mouth is physically tired from smiling and thanking everyone. Just when I'm sure the party is over, Sunny stands and walks out of the room.

While he's gone, Anna calls after him, "Hang on! Let me cover her eyes!"

My eyebrows draw in as I frown. "Anna…"

"Shush, you. Let us do this." She walks over and puts her tiny hands over my eyes, and says, "Now, Sun."

There's a scrapping sound as something, I assume heavy and cardboard, is dragged across the concrete floor. When it stops moving, Anna releases her hold on my eyes. I open them to see the most beautiful white crib. It's on a cardboard box that's been cut open to lay flat. This is apparently the surface it was painted on as there are flecks, spills, and lines from the white paint used on it.

I stand and walk over to inspect it. The small crowd is quiet as I walk around it, dragging my hand over all the rails. I look at Sunny. "Is this…"

His smile is broad and proud. "It is. It was yours, and then the twins' crib. I've spent the last few weeks refinishing it."

"But where did you..."

Sunny shifts awkwardly. "Your, uh, Dad gave it to me for you."

I gape. "How? When did you see him? How did he know? I haven't been to visit."

Sunny smiles sweetly and winks at me. "We'll talk later, kiddo."

I start to cry the tears I've been fighting to hold back all day. "Thank you, Sunny. This is amazing." As I take in the faces of the people who are here for me in this moment, it feels like "thank you" isn't enough. It's not. This is an impossible situation. This is a baby that isn't supposed to be. I messed up Rhae's life. Ryan fucking died. It all becomes too much, and I start to feel light-headed. Someone must have noticed because as I begin to sway on my feet, sure I'm about to hit the floor, arms come around me and lower me to the floor slowly.

"Dammit, Sunny!" Anna fusses. "I knew this would be too much on her today."

Sunny's voice sounds frustrated. "Anna, there's no way I could have known this would happen."

Irma shuts them both up. "Hush now! The both of ya. Cade, you got her?"

I look around and see Cade is the person who kept me from falling over. All I can manage is a whisper, "I'm sorry."

He nods. "Are you okay?"

"I'm fine. Maybe some punch? That should help."

Anna fusses at me for everything from not eating right to not taking my pre-natal vitamins to finally landing on my blood pressure issues. I don't argue with her. I learned a long time ago that you don't fuss with Anna. If I let her have her say, the moment will pass faster. Rhae brings me a tiny cup of punch, and I start sipping. I can feel myself getting stronger, but it's not that I'm stronger. The onslaught of emotions has passed. I'm getting things back under control. Eventually, Cade and Sunny help me off the floor.

Before long, everyone is helping load my haul into Cade's truck. He and Rhae have agreed to take the stuff to the house and put it in the nursery for me. Knowing how Ryan described their own struggles with fertility, I worry what being in that house with a room setup as a nursery will do to Rhae. Cade is with her, and it could be good for her to go back one more time. She's a tougher cookie than even her family ever knew. I've learned how tough, and what a big heart she has when she gave me the house. Rhae likes to keep it hidden, but she's like Sunny—a big softy. I hug them both and thank them for taking my gifts to the house. Rhae squeezes me extra hard when she says, "Of course. We'll get it all set up for you. Then you can change it."

Anna doesn't want me to work my shift, but Sunny

believes I'm capable of making my own decisions. They talk about for a bit, but eventually she gives up. She makes me agree to call her if I feel anything strange.

I can't help but joke, "So baby feet in my ribcage—weird or normal? It feels weird, but I'm told it's totally normal."

"Smartass."

I accept that title. If Anna stoops to cussing you, you have really done something.

~

Sunny and I start prepping the bar stock, and the kitchen staff arrives to get food together for tonight.

"Have you hired another bartender yet?" I ask Sunny.

He nods. "Yep. She'll be here in a little bit."

"Oh, Thank God. I don't think I could handle any more short-handed Saturday nights."

"I know. Getting her in here on a Wednesday, though, you should have her trained up before we get to the weekend. She's got good experience. I also hired a bar-back," he tells me.

I freeze, "Seriously?" He's never had a bar-back before.

At this, Sunny stops working and smiles at me. "Seriously. It's high-time we both quit trying to kill ourselves up here. Plus, you might be able to train the bar-back to tend bar. They can cover while you're on leave."

"Wow. That's a really, uhm, mature decision, Sunny. Frankly, I'm shocked."

He laughs, and I head back to the ladies' room to make sure it's got toilet paper for the evening. Lord knows, if I'm training, I won't have time to do this kind of thing.

I hear the front door ding as someone comes in, and then Sunny is calling me to the front. The new bartender must be here. Although I think I'm moving quickly, I'm apparently not. My walking style has become more of a waddle, and it's hassling to get anywhere in any reasonable amount of time. When I round the corner, Jess is shaking hands with Sunny.

"What's up, Jess? Did you forget something?"

She exchanges a conspiratorial smile with Sunny. "I'm the new bartender," she says excitedly.

"Shut the front door! No, you aren't. You love being a stay-at-home mom. What happened?"

She smiles at my assumption. "Nothing happened. It's called life. Christmas is coming, and Connor is in a dry spell for extra work hours. I'm going to work nights when he's home. He works days when I'm home. That way someone is with the kids all the time, and we can save up."

Jess doesn't realize that I know all too well what that's like. I watched Mama do the same thing when it came time for my own Christmas and back-to-school clothes. Not to mention how she worked to provide for Thanksgiving and birthdays.

73

"It's good to have you! Someone I know can wait tables, tend bar, and have my back when I need it. Welcome!" I hug her enthusiastically.

Sunny says, "Stop the hippie shit and get busy."

We both laugh, and then Jess asks, "Is he always so chipper?"

She and I start going over the cocktail menu, and then the register system we use. As I'm covering the procedures for running a tab, the door dings again. I glance up and feel my heart drop into my feet. *What the actual...* Sunny comes to the front and interrupts my thought. "Jess, Mel, this is Clayton. He's going to be your bar-back and help me with security sometimes."

Clayton smiles at me. "Close your mouth, Mel."

Jess lets out an obnoxious chuckle, and I snap my mouth closed. I'm dumbfounded watching Jess introduce herself to him. There's a million thoughts in my mind, yet when he shakes my hand, I've still got nothing.

Sunny blusters, "We open in less than an hour. Jess, wipe down the tables. Melody, show Clayton to the stock room and tell him what you need to get started. I'm going to my office."

Stunned, I blink a few times before saying, "Uh, this way." I lead Clayton to the stockroom and start by explaining, "Wednesday night customers are like a bunch of old hound dogs. They want to bark and chase rabbits, but they don't have the energy to actually do it. So, I expect lots of bottled beer and Hank

74

on the jukebox."

Clayton laughs. "Okay, so a typical bar."

"Sort of. Don't let me run out of any whiskey either and we should be good."

~

What I told Clayton to expect comes back to bite me in the ass. Hard. I could not have been more wrong! The crowd is not the typical Wednesday crew. There are tons of guys here from the community college. Jess is running drinks to the tables on the floor while I handle the bar itself. She's been helping keep up with drink orders, and I'm even more thankful she's the help Sunny hired. She is freaking amazing at what she does!

"Jess!" I call her over. "What's up with the college guys tonight?"

"Oh, mid-terms just wrapped up. They're celebrating."

I roll my eyes. "I lost track of time. Again. Need anything?"

"Naw, baby. I got it. You do you, boo."

I laugh, and turn to close out a tab.

"You have a baby...in a bar," someone says behind me.

I stop what I'm doing, and turn around. The guy leaning on the bar that looks remotely familiar. I glare at him and return to finish with the register. "What can I get you, sir?" I ask in my normal bartender voice.

He chuckles. "Don't you get it? Didn't you see that movie?"

"What movie?"

"Ugh. C'mon that line would have been way funnier if you had seen that movie. Shit, what was the name of that movie? Blonde actress, goes off to the big city and has to come home to get her small-town husband to sign divorce papers."

The wheels spinning in his head are almost tangible. I worry he might blow a gasket trying to think of the name of that movie. I take pity on him. "It's not important. So yeah, baby in a bar." I point at my belly. "Funny. What can I get for you?"

His smile is regretful. "Yeah, sorry. Bad jokes are bad. I'll have a soda."

"That's a real party animal for ya. Drinking soda all night." I mimic the party guys when I end my sarcastic statement by yelling, "Woo-hoo!"

"I would think, of all people, a bartender would understand the designated driver concept."

"Whatever. One soda, coming right up." I use the spray nozzle on the bar to fill a cup of ice with the soda he requested, then push it across the counter to him. "Shall I start a tab for you?"

Before he can answer, Clayton joins me behind the bar. He's loading more beer into the rapid cooler.

The guy I've been poking fun at says, "Hey Bro! What are you doing here?" At first, I think he's talking to one of his college buddies, but then Clayton stops working and says, "Do I need to clock out to babysit you, Trey?"

Faking offense, Trey says, "Of course not. Ask little mama there, I'm drinking soda."

"*Oh!* I see! You're the guy Clayton had to pick up from the ladies' room that night! You're his brother, Trey!"

He smiles shyly. "That's me. Sorry about that, by the way." He finishes with a grimace.

"You look very different standing upright."

"Aw, shucks. You're too pretty to say things like that to me." Poor guy's cheeks are turning pink.

"Whatever, dude. Why don't you play something non-frat boy on the jukebox," I tease.

Trey smiles, slides off the bar stool and says, "Yes, ma'am."

Clayton leans down to my ear, "Thanks. He really is a good kid. He gets messed up sometimes."

I smile but don't look at him. "Let's just say, I recognize the type. It's no big deal."

He wraps an arm around my shoulders and gives me a squeeze. "It's a big deal to me." That brief contact leaves me feeling cold when he lets go and walks away.

"Clayton," I say to get his attention.

"Yeah, Mel?"

"Sorry I was a bitch at the garage. I'm out of control lately. I never apologized for that, so..." I trail off.

He smiles. "Let's say, I recognize the type. What if we tried to press reset and be friends?"

I smile conspiratorially. "You think that's a good idea?"

He reaches a hand out to me. "Let's shake on it. Friends, okay?"

Let's test the waters of friendship. "Friends help friends paint."

His raucous laughter fills the bar and causes more than a few heads to turn. "You *still* haven't painted the nursery?"

Defiantly, I shake my head. "Nope. Bought the paint though." I'm proud I got that far. I lift my chin proudly.

His smile is knowing when he says, "Friends help friends paint. Just tell me when and where."

Chapter 6

Handyman

Clayton is coming over to help paint the nursery today. I'm up early because I'm nervous as hell. He's the first person, not family in one way or another that I've invited to my tiny, new home. I don't know him that well, but I get the feeling that he's a good guy. I call Sunny to ask him to come check on me while Clayton is here today.

"Make it look like a surprise check-in," I tell him as I lay out my plan.

"Melody, why would you invite this guy to your house? You don't know anything about him," Sunny fusses.

"I have a good feeling about him, okay. We're friends."

Sunny makes a disgusting noise that starts in the back of his throat.

"Besides, you hired him to work in the bar. You must like

him, too. Just be a good dad and come check on me, okay?"

"Fine," he agrees, "but you need to know I have a ride scheduled today. So I won't be alone."

I laugh. "Even better. Will you bring me jalapeño peppers?"

Sunny chuckles. "You are so weird."

I finish getting dressed in an old, baggy T-shirt and some maternity leggings. It's a terrible look, but I honestly don't have any other clothes I can ruin with painting. I wrap my long blonde hair up on top of my head in a messy bun. Well, it wouldn't be messy if I didn't make it look messy on purpose. But I don't want to make it look like I'm trying too hard. As I'm pulling some small tendrils of hair out of the bun, right over my ears, and using a tiny bit of gel to give them some curl, the doorbell rings.

I glance at the clock on my nightstand, and know it has to be Clayton. He is precisely on time, arriving at ten o'clock as agreed. I waddle-walk to the front door and can see his silhouette standing on the other side. Looking at the microwave clock in the kitchen, I decide to wait to answer the door.

At 10:02 a.m., I open the door for him. "Good morning. You're late."

He tries to glare at me, but he's too adorable to pull it off. "I'm not. You stood there until I was late before you answered the door." He raises his eyebrows at me.

"You saw me?"

Clayton shakes his head. "Nope. I saw the other pregnant lady standing on your side of the door."

I roll my eyes. "Oh. You saw my shadow."

"Just remember that if you can see mine, I can see yours." His smile is devilish.

He makes my knees weak, and I have an urge to reach out and feel his beard, but I restrain myself by folding my arms over the baby.

He interrupts my wayward mind when he says, "Show me this nursery that you can't manage to get painted."

"Should I even try to explain that it's not that I can't manage to get it painted? I mean I know how, but pregnant ladies and painting, fumes and stuff?"

He shakes his head. "Are you unable to admit when you need help? Is this a pride thing?"

"No. I'm independent."

"Ah. I get it. Show me."

"Right this way." I walk him to the back bedroom and open the door. "Ta-da!" I say as I walk in ahead of him. The things from the baby shower are all in here, haphazardly arranged in the middle of the room so we can get to the walls. It looks like storage instead of a nursery.

Clayton doesn't bat an eye at all of it. He walks around the edges, inspecting the walls. Running his flattened hand over each wall as far as he can reach up and back down all the way to the floor. When he completes the entire room this way, he stands by me with his hands on his hips. He makes the standard man face when they're about to produce an extremely educated proclamation. After a moment, he says, "Two coats of paint shouldn't take more than half a day in a room this size. Did you want to repair any of the nail holes in the walls?"

I'm a little stunned by his assessment of the job and the room. "No?"

He smiles down at me. "Is that a question or an answer?"

I shrug. "I don't know. What's typical in this situation? Fix the holes or don't?"

He laughs. "Relax, Melody. I'm not here to steal your virtue or judge your decisions. If you want to fix the holes, we need spackle, and it will take time to let the spackle dry so we can sand it. It's a bit more time if you decide to go that way."

"Fine. No. I'm good with tiny holes in the walls."

"Cool. Show me these supplies you apparently picked up."

I point at the paint cans in the far corner of the room. Until this very moment, I was feeling pretty proud of the fact that I thought to buy the things Jim suggested.

Clayton squats to look at everything and then looks back at

me. "No drop cloth?"

"Well, I wasn't sure what I needed, so I went to see Jim at the hardware store. He put all the supplies together for me. Do we need a drop cloth?"

He smirks. "You have a roller and replacement roller heads, and he even got you a brush to cut-in with. Looks like the only thing we need is the drop cloths."

"I can run to the store if you want to get started," I offer.

"Nope. We'll go together. My treat."

Before I can argue, he stops me by holding up his hand. "It's only a couple drop cloths and some labor. My gift to you and the baby. Let's go."

I'm speechless when he takes me by the hand and leads me to the door. I'm still stunned when he hands me my purse from the table by the door and says, "I'll drive. We can take my truck."

We drive to the hardware store, and he rambles on about how he messed up the day I got the oil change as we walk toward the painting section of the store. The only thing I hear is the apology he makes, but it must be the second or third time he says it because he's looking at me like a lost child. "Hey, Melody, you in there? What's up?"

"Oh, sorry. I don't know. I check out sometimes. What were you saying?"

He smiles, sweetly. "I was saying I'm sorry for the way I asked those questions about the baby's dad. I didn't mean to be offensive or pry into your business. I know I hurt your feelings."

I shake my head. "There's nothing to apologize for. I shouldn't be so sensitive about it."

He nods. "Okay, we're good then?"

"Yep. All good."

~

Clayton is meticulous about his setup for painting. He's carefully taped off all the trim around the doors and windows. He's spread a drop cloth over the baby shower stuff, which he has organized into a tighter pile in the middle of the room. He asked me to open the window to vent some of the fumes. Next, he spreads the drop cloth on the floor to protect the carpet.

"This carpet is practically new," he observes. "It's like whoever put it in closed this room up and never used it."

"Well," I start, then sigh. "They kind of did. The people who used to live here wanted kids, but they weren't able to have any. So it was just the two of them until..." I trail off wondering how much of this story I should share. I know that talking about Ryan will eventually lead to sharing about my past with him and how I came into the house. I decide not to go on.

"Until what?" he asks.

I look up at him. "Ah, nothing. That's a story for another

time."

"I don't know if you noticed, but we have all day to paint this room and talk."

I let out a small, nervous laugh. "Okay, we need a radio."

He's pouring paint in the tray and chuckles. "Now, why do we need a radio?"

"It takes the pressure off people thinking they need to talk. Plus, baby boy likes music."

He sobers and looks over his shoulder at me. "I thought you didn't know. It's a boy?"

I shrug. "I think so. I can't afford the ultrasound to find out for sure, but I'm almost certain it's a boy."

He nods and gets back to paint setup. "All right, Melody. Go grab a radio, but we will circle back to that conversation you don't want to have right now.

He has no idea why that scares me to the bone. My biggest fear is someone else knowing and judging me. It was hard enough to bring Anna and Sunny into the whole thing, but to keep spreading that knowledge around is just unbearable. I'm always prepared for everyone else to judge me harder than I judge myself. I haven't actually worked through what it might be like to trust someone and own it as my past, not my present. But, then again, it is my present, too.

This baby is part of that. A part I can't deny forever. When we're on the outside of the situation, we think we have all the answers about what they should or should not do, and how much better *our* decisions would be in that situation. No one knows what it's like to be that person and make those decisions until they're in that moment themselves. I never thought it would be me.

~

Clayton is putting a plastic grocery sack over the roller, and a separate bag over the pan of paint. I was critical of him pouring so much paint when he was close to finishing the first coat, but I'm trying to be trusting of his process.

"What now?" he asks.

I shrug, "What do you mean what now? We watch paint dry. Don't we?"

He shakes his head. "That sounds boring. Show me the rest of the house."

"Son, that better not be code for sex," Sunny's gruff voice cuts in before I can answer.

Clayton turns and the part of his cheeks not covered with beard start turning pink. "No, sir. Mr. Davis, how are you?" He offers his hand to Sunny for a handshake. I'm watching the interaction cautiously.

Sunny's cutting his eyes at Clayton, but shakes the offered hand. "Mr. Davis was my daddy. I'm Sunny. You remember that, boy."

"Yes, sir."

"Is this your handiwork?"

Clayton smiles. "It is. Just the first coat, though."

His eyes narrow. "Melody, you didn't fix the nail holes in the walls?"

I shrug. "It would take extra time. I kind of get the feeling that we're running out of time on this project, Sunny."

He chuckles. "I hope so. You're a mean pregnant woman."

Clayton starts to laugh with him but stops short when I cut my eyes at him. "Mel, where's your bathroom?"

I point down the hall and turn back to Sunny when he leaves the room. "I'm mean?"

He laughs. "Naw, baby. How's this thing with the boy going? Do you need me to stay?"

I shake my head. "No. I think he's good people. We're okay. I thought you said you wouldn't be alone today."

"I'm meeting Max when I leave here. Do you need money? I know these supplies weren't cheap."

"Nope."

Sunny turns his head like a confused puppy. "Really?"

I nod. "All good. Jim at the hardware store took good care

of me."

"Fair enough. I'm going on my ride now. Call if you need anything, okay?"

From the front room, I hear Clayton gasp. "Sunny, is that your motorcycle on the curb?"

"Of course it is," he answers and looks at me. "He's a bit simple, ain't he?" He's laughing as he points to his own head.

"Sunny! Don't say things like that!" I chastise as we walk to the front room where Clayton is staring out the window.

Sunny and I say our goodbyes, and Clayton admires the motorcycle a bit more closely before Sunny pulls away from the curb. I step back into the nursery to see if the paint is drying. I'm staring hard, but I can't tell one way or the other.

I look around the house for Clayton to ask him if it's been long enough, but I can't find him. As I pass through the living room, there's movement out on the back porch. I look out to see Clayton playing with a cat on my porch.

I open the door, and he turns laughing. "Hey, I love your cat. What a sweetheart!"

"I don't have a cat."

He stops laughing and stares at the cat as if the cat is going to give him any answers. Thinking it over for a moment, he asks, "Don't you want a cat? He's great."

I can't help but laugh at him. What a doofus. Totally

adorable. "Uh, no. I'm good. Are you hungry?"

The look of satisfaction on his face is endearing. "God, I thought you'd never bring up lunch. I'm starved. What are we eating?"

I didn't expect his enthusiasm, and I tell him so. "Truthfully, I'm always hungry these days. So, I was hoping it was meal time. I was actually waiting on you to say something. Let's see what I have in the kitchen. We might have to make a run for sub sandwiches or something."

Together we walk into the kitchen. Clayton is the consummate, chivalrous guy. He opens doors, closes them behind me. He looks in the upper cabinets that I need a step-stool to get into. I look through the fridge. We both come to the same conclusion. Either we go out for lunch, or its tomato sandwiches and plain chips. I study him as he looks me over.

"Hmmmm, you don't look like you want to go out for food," he observes.

"And you have paint in your hair. 'Mater sandwiches it is!" I declare.

We are a like a choreographed assembly line. Working perfectly together, each with their own task that picks up where the other left off. We just know what the other wants, and anticipate when to act.

Clayton lays out paper plates with slices of bread. I follow behind him with mayo on each slice. Clayton comes behind me, slicing tomatoes without a cutting board. He holds the tomato in his hand and uses a paring knife to slice off thin pieces onto each sandwich. After he finishes, I salt and pepper the tomatoes. Clayton comes in behind me as he closes each sandwich. When he does, I put a few chips on each plate.

Finally, he hands me a paper towel for my plate as he covers his own. He picks up the plates, stacking one on top of the other, and tells me to grab two cups with ice water. I'm smiling like an idiot as I follow him to the back door. He's left one hand free so he can operate the doorknob for us. There's a picnic table set out under the shade tree at the bottom of the porch stairs. This is where we sit down to have our lunch on a rare, sunny, early spring day.

I'm starting to think about the 'what if' questions concerning Clayton. What if he sees me as more than a friend? What if I want more than friendship with him? I almost forget about all the guilt with Ryan and the baby, and start to enjoy being with someone new. He's so fun to be around, and we seem to be on the same level in terms of humor and what we expect from other people. But I still don't know him that well. When we finish our sandwiches, I decide that since he knows a little about me, maybe I can drag some information out of him.

"So, Gulf Shores," I start.

Clayton nods. "Yep. Born and raised down there. Have you ever been?"

I shake my head. "Nope, but I know it's a beach town

down on the coast. Why in the world would you move here when you were already living in paradise?"

He sighs. "I guess that depends on your definition of paradise."

Taking a drink of water, I think over his point. "Okay, so what's your definition of paradise?"

Clayton swallows the chips he's eating. "I don't know. I just know Gulf Shores is most people's definition of paradise, and I'm kind of over it. Ya know? It's a resort town that is really a small town undercover. I needed to get away and see what the rest of the world was like. This picnic is fairly close to paradise, I think."

"Oh," I say. "I was thinking sand, sun, fun, and all that was paradise. Silly me."

We both laugh off the awkwardness of the conversation.

"I'm sorry. Home has a lot of bad memories for me. I came up here to escape a girlfriend who cheated on me. She was tired of my lack of ambition. When I wasn't what she wanted anymore, she started hooking up with this rich guy. I found out, and if there's one thing I can't tolerate, it's a cheater."

"Wow." He would hate my story, then. It was a good decision not to tell him about Ryan.

Clayton laughs again. "Yeah, so I called my brother, Trey. You've met, right?"

I'm emotionless when I answer. "Yeah, I guess."

His laugh is deep. "Everything fell apart right after he moved up here to work for Miles Construction, and he offered to let me crash with him. I took him up on the offer. Old man Busby needed a mechanic because he got tired of turning wrenches and wanted to run the office again. Next thing I know, I'm meeting a gorgeous bartender." He winks.

I feel sick to my stomach when he does. He can't stand cheaters, and I participated in an extramarital affair. I'm no better than his ex. He wouldn't even want to be friends with me if he knew the truth.

"So, tell me more about the father of your baby," Clayton says.

My answer is simple. "Nope." This is not a conversation I'm ready to have with him.

Chapter 7

Lyric Jane

After our picnic lunch, which was full of revelations about both Clayton and myself, I decided to keep things with him cool. I didn't tell him the truth when I had the chance to do it. Instead, we talked through the evening as he put the second coat of paint on the nursery. I went to bed that night feeling like the lowest piece of shit ever. *Why didn't I tell him? What harm could it have done?* He would have to make a decision about his stance on cheaters.

I couldn't bear the thought of him seeing me as a dirty, lying, cheater. Still, I was weak and gave him my number when he asked for it. That was two weeks ago. He calls me daily to check on how I'm feeling. All I want to do when I hear his genuine, sweet voice is confess the whole truth. Thankfully, I haven't caved to that compulsion yet.

When he comes to visit, it's always under the premise of fixing up things around the house. He's repaired a not-so-squeaky door, rebuilt the porch steps out back, and stopped my toilet from running in the middle of the night. I'm selfish enough that I enjoy having him around. The more time we spend together, the more intimate he becomes. He holds me when I'm tired. He rubs my back when I say it's bothering me. We watch movies and eat popcorn like old friends.

I'm an idiot for allowing this to continue. It's going to end badly, but I can't help myself. I like having someone find me attractive, especially at this stage in my pregnancy. Mostly, I feel like I have a closer likeness to a beluga whale than to a woman.

The baby is continually trying to stretch out, and there isn't any more room for either of us. He is killing my bladder, and I'm short of breath when he really stretches. I'm no doctor, but I think the baby squishes my lungs when that happens.

Today is my checkup. I'm thirty-six weeks with forever to go. "I'm miserable all the time," I tell Dr. Peterson. "Can't you go ahead and take the baby early? Induce labor. Something. Anything. I can't keep living like this."

Dr. Peterson laughs at me. He *laughs* at me. "Melody, do you know how many women beg me to induce labor early? It's not good for the baby. Try to think of that when it gets hard."

"I do try, but then I remember how miserable I am. I want this baby out. It's been hard for months now."

He laughs at me again. "You only have four more weeks. Are you feeling less anxious about the delivery, then?"

I nod, then shrug. "Yes. No."

The idea of living this way for four more weeks makes me cry. So, I try not to think about it. I decide to go grocery shopping on my way home from the doctor's appointment. I dread doing this because I would rather eat with Anna and Sunny than buy groceries and cook.

Anna and Sunny aren't home, though. They decided to take a short trip before the baby comes so that they can be there for me. Really, it's a weekend getaway on the two weekdays the bar is closed. I encouraged them to go.

They do so much to look after the twins and me, they deserve the break. They sent the boys to Jess for the week. She's been a blessing I never imagined, too.

I'm buying groceries when my phone starts to ring. I check it to see that Clayton is calling. I decide not to answer. I don't want any further reminders of how shitty I am as a human being today. *Stop being melodramatic.* I turn down the next aisle, and my phone starts ringing again. Clayton, again. He just won't give up.

I answer, "Hey."

"Hey, yourself. I like those leggings."

I stop walking when he says this and look down. Of course, I can't see the leggings so I stick my left leg out to the side to see which pair I wore today. Then I realize that he's on the phone, not with me. God, my brain is seriously slow these days. I close my eyes and turn my face to the ceiling. Then I slowly lift the phone back to my ear. "Where are you?"

"Right here." His voice is in the ear that isn't glued to the phone. Goosebumps raise up on every inch of my skin. I end the call, put the cell phone back in my purse, then lean against him. My face is buried in his chest, breathing in his scent. I wish I didn't find such comfort in him.

Clayton leans down and whispers in my ear, "I really like the skull and roses look."

I smile. "I like these, too. Look, Clayton, we have to talk." The guilt of not telling him the truth about everything is starting to weigh me down. It's probably hormones, but I need to get some things out in the open.

He hugs me and puts his small basket into my buggy. "Okay, let's talk. Are you done shopping?"

I nod. "Yeah. Frozen meals are all I have the energy to cook lately. I get the big buggy so I can lean on it as I walk."

"Poor thing. Let's get you home. I'll pay for the groceries. You go ahead and drive to the house. I'll be there shortly."

Again, I'm selfish enough to let him buy my groceries and bring them home to me.

When he gets to the house, he knocks as he walks in. This has been developing the more time we spend together. It's almost as if he thinks he lives here. It's irritating and comfortable all at the same time. He starts putting groceries away as soon as he comes in.

I'm sitting at the kitchen table with a glass of water. I can't drink too much at one time, so I sip a lot these days. The irony of sitting at the same table I was at when I told Rhae about the baby isn't lost on me. Here I am, once again, delivering terrible news.

"What did you want to talk about," he asks.

"When you finish putting the stuff away, come sit with me, and we'll talk."

"Okay, honey," he says offhandedly. As soon as the words leave him, he looks at me. He seems a little panicked.

At the same time, I sit up a little straighter and roll the term around in my mouth. I'm not sure how I feel about it. *Am I his honey?*

"Listen, Clayton, we, uh, we've moved a little too..." I stop talking because Clayton's face shifts to a more shocked look. Surprised at this change, I ask, "What?"

"Melody, did your water break?"

I look down at the glass in front of me. "Nope. All good here."

He presses his lips together as a smile tries to spread across his face. "No. Not that water."

I reach down between my legs, and sure as shit, my leggings are wet. I snap my gaze up to his. "What do we do?"

He doesn't even try to control it now; he laughs as a radiant smile breaks through. "Honey, I think we should go to the hospital. Do you have a bag packed?"

"Stop calling me honey," I bite back at him. I don't have anything ready. Tears prick my eyes as I begin to panic. I just saw the doctor. This wasn't supposed to happen for four more weeks. "What's happening?" My voice becomes shrill. My face heats and my breathing accelerates. I'm about to have a full-blown panic attack.

Clayton rushes over to me and takes my face in his hands. "Calm down. This is normal. There's no reason to panic."

I nod and try to control my breathing when a contraction hits. It's painful but only lasts a few seconds. Clayton leads me to the bedroom and does exactly what I say about packing some things for the baby and me. He gives me his arm and helps me out the door and down the stairs to his truck. As soon as I'm settled, he takes my keys and locks the front door. By the time he's back to the truck, I'm crying because I'm scared of what's about to happen. When your water breaks, they have to keep you in the hospital and deliver the baby. *It's too soon.*

Clayton drives like a calm old man. During the drive, he keeps murmuring soothing things to me. "It's okay. This is a good thing. Breathe through it." I'm still quietly panicking and wishing he would drive faster. But I know he's trying to be safe. He reaches over and takes my hand. His presence is calming as he rubs circles with his thumb into the back of my hand.

As I begin to relax, another contraction starts. I can't remember if I should be doing something constructive or helpful like timing the contractions. I don't know whether I'm supposed to time how far apart the contractions are or how long they last. Both? Before I can get too wound up about it, Clayton pulls into the ambulance bay at the emergency room. A security guard runs out to tell him he can't park there, when he interrupts her by telling her that my water broke. Without another word, she runs back inside.

I continue focusing on my breathing while Clayton helps to get out of the truck. The security guard returns with a wheelchair. I'm thankful I won't have to walk through this contraction.

Everything starts to happen faster and becomes a blur. I nod when I'm supposed to and answer questions like a robot. Clayton gets my phone out of my purse and steps into the hallway. I'm terrified to be alone, but the nurses are still connecting me to monitors and starting IVs. Before I know it, Dr. Peterson is walking into the room with Clayton right behind him.

I can't help but hold my hand out for Clayton when he walks into the room. He takes my hand and sits on the bed beside me. I start to ask if he got in touch with Anna, and he shushes me. "Hang on one second," he says. I follow his gaze. He's staring at the monitor that shows the baby's heartbeat. "Look at that. How freaking cool is this? Are you ready?" He's smiling down at me, and I'm not smiling.

"Clayton, you can't be here. I'm a liar. I need to tell you the truth about the baby's dad before he's born."

He looks puzzled. "What are you talking about, Melody? You need me, I can't leave you right now."

Dr. Peterson interrupts, "Wait, this isn't the baby's father?"

I shake my head. "Not now, doc. Clayton, listen to me..." Before I can finish what I'm trying to say, a serious contraction starts. Clayton winces as I nearly break his fingers, squeezing his hand. Frustrated by hormones and pain, I growl. "Clayton, get out. You aren't the baby's father. You and I are not together. Leave."

He looks at me with a great betrayal in his eyes. My heart breaks into a million pieces, but I can't help it. This was always what was going to happen.

"Don't do this, Melody. You can't do this alone. It's the hormones talking. You don't mean that."

I growl at him again. "I mean it! We aren't even dating," I spit the words at him. "I'm not alone. There are doctors and nurses."

"But, Mel, don't..."

"Dr. Peterson, get him out! Now!"

Dr. Peterson is staring at me over the tented sheet with his mouth wide open. "Melody, you need a partner to help you push. Are you sure?"

"Then get me a nurse. He's out!"

Clayton gives my hand one last squeeze, imploring me to look at him. I scrunch my eyes closed tight and refuse. My heart is shattering, my body is wracked with pain, and I know I'm acting like a small child. It's as if I'm floating above the scene as it's unfolding. My spirit is screaming at me to stop acting a fool, but my brain refuses to give in.

He gives my hand a tiny pat. "Please, Melody. Look at me," he whispers. I still refuse to speak to him. Finally, he lets go of my hand. Fat, hot tears roll down my face as I fight the urge to tell him to stay. When I hear the door of the room open, I open my eyes. His shoulders are hunched as he stands with the door open. Then he turns to me once more. His eyes are full of unshed tears. I don't ask him to stay. I must make him leave.

The look on his face as he walks out is going to haunt me. I've ruined him. Regret floods my system, and it is a bitter feeling. I'm too proud to take it back. It's better this way. It was always destined to end badly for us. He's nothing to me. I'm nothing to him.

I can't focus on Clayton much longer. There are so many contractions that I've lost track of time. The nurse that takes Clayton's place by my bed introduces herself as Marie. She's young with dark curly hair, and for some reason, all I can think is that Marie is the wrong name for her. Marie is a mean old lady, and this girl is so young and kind.

I follow the instructions as Dr. Peterson and Marie give them to me. Breathing through contractions and preparing to push happens in an instant and takes forever at the same time. Time has no concept for me, and I think it's because of the drugs Dr. Peterson allowed me to have. I didn't get the option of an epidural.

Marie starts removing the pillow from behind my back and is supporting me with her body. "It's time to push now, Melody. I'm going to help you. On the next contraction, we're going to push for a count of ten. Are you ready?"

I release a nervous laugh. "Uh yeah, sure. No turning back now."

Marie smiles encouragingly. "You've got this."

Dr. Peterson grabs my ankles, one at a time, and positions my feet in the stirrups. He smiles up at me. "You've got this, Mel."

Just as Marie said, with the next contraction they start coaching me on pushing. It takes three contractions for me to figure out what muscles I need to use to push. Each time, Marie talks me through what I'm feeling and how to adjust where I'm pushing.

I'm exhausted when Dr. Peterson stands up from the foot of the bed and peeks over the sheet at me. "Melody, I know you're ready to give up. Just a couple more pushes and we'll have a baby. Dig deep and find some strength for me. We need you right now. This baby needs you, Mama."

I nod. When Marie can see the next contraction start on the monitor, she tells me to push harder than I have been. I'm holding my breath as she counts to ten slowly. When the contraction lets up, I fall against the bed heaving. That was the hardest push so far. Marie mops sweat off my face, and asks, "Have you picked out names yet?"

"A few," I pant.

Marie watches the monitor. "Well, what are they? On this next push, you're going to have that sweet baby in your arms. Best be ready." Her hands are rubbing circles on my arms. When the next contraction starts she says, "Okay, Mama. Last push. Let's give it everything you have."

My body is so exhausted that I don't think I can push anymore. But before I can argue with her, she's sliding her arm under my back and whispering encouragements about how strong I am. "You are stronger than you think you are. Do it for this baby. Find something deep down and push!"

I push as hard as I can. All of my strength, all of the pain, all of the secrets, all of the resentment, all of my fears—everything. I push it all into the contraction. The burn that tears through me is suddenly unimportant compared to the joy that fills the room when I hear my baby cry. I start crying, too. It's a cry, but it's the most beautiful sound I've ever heard. That beautiful noise is coming from a person I made.

Despite my greatest fears of delivering a baby, despite the memories of losing my mama when she delivered the twins, despite fear of the unknown, I just pushed a new life into this world. The emotions are overwhelming. My pants turn to sobs as I stretch my arms toward the baby in the doctor's arms.

Dr. Peterson announces, "She's seven pounds, twelve ounces, and twenty-two inches long."

I sober. "Did you say 'she?'"

Marie walks over to my bed with a bundle of blankets and leans down, placing the baby in my arms. "She's beautiful. Lots of hair, Mama."

Still in disbelief that Irma nailed this whole gender thing, I peel the blankets back to get a good look at my daughter. She's real. She's really real. She's here in my arms. I stare into that sweet, chubby, face with the greasy stuff on her eyes, and I know exactly what to name her.

～

Less than twenty-four hours later, I have a hospital room full of visitors. Jess brought the twins and her two kids. Sunny and Anna arrived at the crack of dawn this morning with Mrs. Irma in tow. I don't know if it's the clearing of the pregnancy fog, but Irma looks sick. Something isn't right.

"Irma, are you feeling okay?" I ask.

"Look who's asking. How are you feeling?" she retorts.

Even though I don't believe her, I smile. "She's beautiful. You nailed it. You knew I was having a girl." I remind myself to check on her again when we're alone. I'm sure she's being ornery because there are so many people here.

Irma shrugs. "It was a fifty-fifty shot."

Everyone in the room erupts in peals of laughter. I smile and kiss my sweet baby's nose.

"Where's Clayton?" Sunny asks. He knows how much time we've spent together in the last several weeks.

I'm not thrilled with him for asking. I've been trying to forget the dramatic fit I threw. "I sent him home."

"When?" he asks. "He called me when you went into labor."

I huff. "I don't want to talk about it."

Sunny doesn't know what to say, so he lets it drop. I'm sure he'll bring it up later, though.

Irma takes over the conversation. "So, what did ya name that baby?"

I look at Anna first and crook my finger, asking her to come closer. I take her hand when she does. "Mel, what is it?"

"Mama was your best friend, Anna. I think of her all the time and remember how you both loved the Beatles. I used to ask her why she loved them so much. Do you remember her answer?"

Anna nods. "I do."

I smile. "She used to say that there was elegance in simplicity and that their most popular tunes were simple. She also used to tell me to pay attention to the lyrics of a song. There is always a message in a song; always a deeper meaning."

Anna's laughter gives way to tears, happy tears. I give her hand a tender tug, and she leans down to hug me. We hold each other closer for a moment. When I look around the room again, there isn't a dry eye in the place.

I smile broadly and wipe away the tears because this is a moment of joy. "I'd like to introduce my daughter, Lyric Jane. She's named for my mother, Jane Richards."

Even the nurse who came in to check on the baby is crying.

Chapter 8

Settling In

"You ready, kid?" Sunny asks as he walks into the hospital room. I was released a few days ago, but they wanted the NICU to observe Lyric for a little while. She was a bit premature, and the doctor was worried she would need extra help. She proved them all wrong. She's nursing well and has the strongest lungs I've heard on a baby.

Sunny came to collect us from the hospital. Dr. Peterson has insisted that I not drive for a few more weeks. He says I need to build my strength back up from the delivery.

"Almost. Let me put a hat on her head," I tell him.

"Okay. I'm going to see if there's anything else for us to sign. You good?"

I nod. "Stop making a fuss and get to hauling."

Sunny laughs and leaves us to finish getting ready. I'm still fussing over her hair and putting her tiny hat on just right. She has a cowlick of hair that swooshes across her forehead in the sweetest way. But it is a pain in my ass to get it tucked under the little hat.

I plant kisses on her chubby little baby belly before putting a pair of pink socks on her feet. Late March is already hotter than I remember any other year being. Still, it could be cool enough to give her a chill. I stare at her sweet, sleeping face and think of Ryan. He would be crazy about her.

Without warning, I think of Clayton. He'd be crazy about her, too. He was crazy about her when I kicked him out of the delivery room. A pain strikes my heart, and I know I did the wrong thing. It was emotional and not thought out. Then a feeling of guilt washes over me. We were getting really close when I went crazy bitch on him. "What's wrong with me?" I ask aloud.

I'm startled when Dr. Peterson says, "I wondered when you were going to get around to beating yourself up about kicking that boy out."

I groan. "Clarity is a bitch."

He laughs. "That, my dear, is an understatement. Good thing we get second chances. And third chances. And…"

"I get it. I didn't expect to see you today. Lyric just got released."

"I heard. Dr. Luz is an old friend of mine. Since you're here, I wanted to come by and see how you're feeling."

I shrug. "Other than like a fool? I'm good. Sometimes I feel like a deflated balloon. I'm ready to start working out and get the weight off, but I know, I have to wait another few weeks."

He nods. "Okay. Sounds like you're thinking clearly. Give that boy a call, will you?"

"Doctor's orders?"

"Yes, ma'am."

~

We arrive home and find Anna, Irma, and Jess sitting on the front porch. I can't help the smile that spreads across my face. "Look, Lyric, the welcoming committee is here to greet you."

Sunny groans. "That's too much for me today. Anna has her car. I'm going to the bar."

Laughing, I tell him, "I'll send Jess your way shortly."

He helps me get out of the truck, and then turns to get Lyric out. Those car carrier things must be safe because the damn things weigh a ton. Add an eight-pound baby to it and it's almost impossible to carry that thing very far. I'm grateful to Sunny for doing the heavy lifting. Before I can express my gratitude, Jess is down the steps, halting Sunny from going up the stairs. She digs around in the carrier and takes Lyric out of it.

Sunny shakes his head. "Crazy women."

Jess uses her free hand to swat him. "Hey. Your wife is among the baby-crazed."

Anna has joined us in the yard. Sunny kisses the top of her head, and hands the carrier to her. He leaves us to be baby-crazed without him. Sunny isn't a super-social guy anyway, so this is par for the course after weeks of being surrounded by people. Chiefly, being surrounded by women. I expected him to crack sooner. I'm actually impressed he lasted this long. So is Anna.

Later, the ladies take turns passing the baby between them. When Lyric has had enough, she lets us know. I take her and retreat to the nursery to nurse her. While I sit in the rocking chair, and absorb the atmosphere and calm of this room, I can't help but think of Clayton again. He worked so hard for someone who treated him like shit. Whispering to Lyric, who is greedily feeding, I tell her, "Mommy is a horrible person. Don't worry; I'm not going to be horrible to you. I was horrible to someone else. I'm done being that person. We can fix this little one."

I rock Lyric after she finishes nursing, and then gently lay her in her crib. It is full of stuffed toys and a folded blanket at the foot. I remove it all. The hospital educators scared me to death about SIDS. I plan to always put her on her back and keep pillows and soft items out of the crib with her. I realize that it's a precaution and not necessarily that every baby could be affected, but I take no chances with my sweet girl. She's irreplaceable.

When I step out of her room, I walk in on Irma telling Jess that she needs to get to work. Anna agrees that Sunny would never fuss at her for being late, but he would kill himself trying to do it all alone so she could spend time with the baby.

Jess stands and hugs every one of us. After she hugs me, she says, "I'll be back." I laugh at her and say, "Please. I'm so freaking sleepy right now. I wouldn't turn down a nap."

Anna walks over to me and says, "We need to work out a rotation to help you through the first few weeks. If we do it all too fast, we'll burn out with you. I'm going to run home and make sure the boys are doing their chores. They're supposed to go visit with your dad some this weekend."

"Kiss them for me. Love you," I say as I hug her goodbye.

Anna looks at me sternly. "I know you just got home with the baby, and I know how you feel about your dad. But honey, he's really doing a lot better this time. You should go see him."

I press my lips into a firm line. "I'll think about it."

She leaves it at that. When she's gone, I look around the room, and it's down to Irma and me. She looks like she has something to say, but she's not acting like herself.

"What's going on, Irma?" I ask.

She sighs. "I can't hide it from everyone. There are a few of my adopted children who can see through me. You happen to be one of them. Are you sure you don't have any gifts?"

When Irma talks about *gifts*, she means the ability to see the future, dreams, reading people, and psychic abilities. All of which Jess, Rhae, Cade, and the others believe Irma possesses. I shake my head slowly as if I'm trying to remember having any of those. Like I could forget. Still, I pretend to think for her sake. "No ma'am. I'm gift-less."

"I just think you refuse to accept your gifts. Ya going to regret that someday. Mark my words, girl. But never-you-mind that. I'm sick, baby."

I outwardly nod in acceptance. Internally, fear spreads through my body down to my fingers and toes. "I figured. How sick?"

She takes a deep breath before starting. I can tell, by the way she knots her hands, it's bad. "Well, baby, they are running tests and everything. The doctor says he thinks it could be cancer. They won't know for sure until the tests come back."

"Mrs. Irma, you know you're going to be fine. They have all kinds of genetic therapy treatments and chemotherapy to help you get well. You're going to kick this in no time," I say trying to be encouraging, but my voice is weak, and I don't even believe it myself. My mind is racing as I try to provide a semblance of comfort for her.

She shakes her head. "Nope. I don't want none of that business. I'm too old and too tired to do all of that jumping through hoops. Nope, my body is tired, and it's telling me it's tired."

I open my mouth to argue with her, but she stops me.

"Don't go telling no one else about this. I'm trusting you, Mel. Now, ya tell me what happened with the boy."

"God, Irma. I don't even know what happened."

"Start from the beginning," she instructs as she settles into the chair.

I take a moment to collect my thoughts. She knows already, and I know it. "I ran him off. I got freaked out, and I ran him off. That's the simplest explanation."

She looks at me dubiously. "Since when does the simple explanation make sense? Get to talking young lady."

"Yes, ma'am. I don't know what got into me. We were hanging out together and having lunch. It was the day he painted the nursery for me. I was asking him about where he was from and why he would move here. I thought they were innocent questions, but he told me about the ex-girlfriend that he had back home, and how they broke up. It was because she cheated on him. He went on a rant about cheaters. How that's the one thing he can't tolerate."

The truth is harder to share than I thought. It takes me several breaths before I manage to go on. "You know how Ryan and I came to make Lyric. It was an affair. It's not something I'm proud of, but I'm a cheater. I couldn't tell him because he would be done with us. It's not like I was conscious of wanting to be with him, but the idea of running him off thinking I'm a cheater made me act crazy."

She looks puzzled. "What do you mean act crazy?"

I shrug. "I didn't tell him anything about Ryan. I want to

tell him. I desperately want to get it all out in the open. If I tell him about Ryan, then I have to own the fact that I had an affair with a married man. And how that affair ended. He wouldn't even want to be my friend if he knew that. It was just nice to be around him, so I didn't tell him. It was selfish."

"How do you figure you were the cheater?" she asks.

"Because when I found out he was married, I didn't call it off. I didn't stop seeing him. That makes me a homewrecker at best."

Irma stands and comes over to join me on the couch. "This is nonsense. Stop beating yourself up for things you can't change. Tell him the damn truth. If he can't handle it, it becomes his problem. Not yours. We clear?"

"Can it really be that simple?" I ask her, disbelief all over my face.

"Of course it can. People are people. We all have our own shit. We all mess up. We all hurt people we care about. The defining moments are when you decide how you gon' fix it. Nothing is beyond repair until we go to the grave. Even then, I have my doubts."

Slowly I nod. "You have a way of seeing things, Mrs. Irma. You are one unique lady, and I'm blessed to have you."

"Yes, you are. Ya only got a couple hours before that sweet baby wakes up hungry again. I'm going to skedaddle on home. Call that boy while ya got the chance."

~

I stare at my phone with Clayton's number pulled up on the screen. Jeez, why is this so freaking hard to do? *Just own your shit, Melody.* I'm mentally chastising myself. *Call him and apologize.*

Irma's right, Lyric will be awake and ready to eat again soon. Before I can think about it anymore, I tap the call button on the screen. The phone seems to ring indefinitely. When I'm sure the call is getting sent to voicemail, he answers.

"Melody?"

I try to speak but nothing comes out. I have to clear my throat. "Yeah. Hey. What's up?" My voice is weak. *What's up? Seriously?*

He takes a moment before responding. Clayton clears his throat, "Not a lot, I guess. How are you?"

"Oh, I'm great. Had a baby. You know, the usual." I'm smiling even thought I know he can't see it.

He chuckles. "There ya go. That sense of humor you're famous for."

I sigh. "Look, Clayton, I need to apologize. The things I said, kicking you out after you've done so much for me. I'm sorry."

He's quiet for a long moment. A moment that stretches for too long.

"Are you still there?" I ask.

"Yeah, I'm still here. Can I see you?" A thrill of excitement burns through me. I try to tamp it down before it can turn into something like hope.

"Please. We have a ton to talk about."

"Give me a few minutes. I need to find a ride. I've had more than a few beers tonight."

My smile fades into a frown. "Don't worry about it then. We'll talk tomorrow when you're clear. This won't be worth it if you're drunk."

"Are you sure?" he asks timidly.

"I'm sure. Let's have breakfast tomorrow morning. I think the baby is going to be up in a little bit anyway. She's always hungry."

He takes a deep breath. "So, it's a girl?"

"Yep."

"What did you name her?"

"Why don't I tell you when you meet her tomorrow morning?" I tease.

He releases a long breath. "I look forward to seeing you both."

Suddenly the loss of him weighs on me heavier than it did before I called. "I know what you mean. Tomorrow, okay?"

"Tomorrow," he agrees.

By the time we're off the phone, I'm remember how exhausted I am. All I want is to fall in the bed. I go in my room and strip for a shower. As I'm about to step in, I catch sight of myself in the full-length bathroom mirror. Things have definitely looked better. I have a pooch of flab where little Ms. Lyric used to make her home. As soon as the doctor gives the all clear, I'm working out. This is ridiculous.

It occurs to me that Lyric might wake up while I shower, but instead of holding off, I jump in and work quickly to get out before she wakes up. I'm congratulating myself on a most efficient use of time when I hear her start to grunt over the baby monitor. I throw a T-shirt over my head quickly and head to the nursery. Before I can get to her, she quiets again. I'm suspicious, so I step in to check on her anyway. She's sleeping peacefully.

I'm finally alone for the first time since she was born. I take advantage of the time by sitting out on the back porch to enjoy the spring night. There's a light breeze that smells sweet, and I think we might have rain tonight. I smile when I hear the distant sound of crickets and locusts. Frogs are ribbiting in the moist night air. I think everything in nature must be mating. Typical spring in the South. Time to make new critters, and bugs.

Usually, I would think that time to let my thoughts run free would be a bad thing, but not tonight. It's an opportunity to think about what I want from life. Do I need someone to help me raise Lyric? I don't think so. I think millions of women have successfully raised their children without any help. I'm sure it's hard as hell, but totally doable.

I'm certain I don't want Clayton in our lives only as a father figure or breadwinner. No, I genuinely miss him. We had the start to a pretty good friendship before I went overthinking everything. Still, I have to play devil's advocate for myself. What if he really can't deal with the truth of who I am or what I did?

I make up my mind that Lyric and I are going to have an amazing life together—with or without Clayton. If he can't see how much I've grown throughout the pregnancy, and that I learned my lessons from being that girl, then he doesn't deserve a chance to be in our lives.

Chapter 9

New Deal

Boom, boom, boom. I sit up in bed. "What the…" I mutter aloud to myself. Then it happens again. I grab my phone to check the time. It's fucking seven a.m. The door. *Oh My God!* Clayton. The baby! I have to resist the urge to yell as I bolt as fast as possible to the door. Yanking it open, I glare at him. "Baby!" It's a scream whisper.

He nearly blushes as he covers his mouth. "Shit. Mel, I'm so sorry. When you said breakfast, I assumed you meant early."

I step aside to let him in and close the door behind him. "Early is relative when there's a new baby trying to get on a routine." I pout as I walk to the nursery and peek in at Lyric who is still sound asleep. Closing her door is a riskier prospect than opening it. Once I'm successful, I walk over to the couch and plop down. It's ungraceful. Then I yank the afghan over me. I immediately start calculating the hours she's been asleep. I fed her at five a.m. and she was back down by six. Looking at the clock, it's seven-thirty a.m. I should have, like, thirty more minutes before she wakes up again.

He chuckles. "No time to dress, then?"

His statement makes me evaluate what I actually have on: panties and a long T-shirt. I shrug. "Who cares anymore? I'm so fucking sleepy. She only sleeps for two hours at a time. Those are cat naps, at best. It feels like forever since I got to sleep through the night. I mean between peeing every ten minutes at the end of the pregnancy to now with how she sleeps or doesn't really," I finish the statement and immediately regret whining. "Dude, I'm sorry. You didn't come over here to hear about my need for sleep. I just..." My apology is interrupted by a serious yawn, which I decide to talk through, "need more than two hours to get some rest. About the time I fall asleep, she starts grunting. Which means it's time to wake up and feed her. I'm starting to feel like a vending machine."

This makes him chuckle. I glare at him, and he stops. "I assume you're breastfeeding."

"You're so smart," I say with thorough sarcasm.

This makes him laugh again. "Okay. Do you have any milk pumped? Any formula?"

"No, and no. I'm not even sure she'll take a bottle."

"Melody." His voice takes on an admonishing tone. "Don't be so quick to shut down solutions. Did you get bottles at the baby shower?"

I nod.

"Did you get a pump?"

I eye him suspiciously. "How are you comfortable having this conversation? I don't feel like talking about breastfeeding and pumping with you."

He shrugs. "I have a sister and a little brother. I have tons of cousins. I've been around a while."

"So you think I should pump some, and then what?"

"Then you take a nice long nap, and I will see to the baby."

Adrenaline spikes in my blood, and I feel my face heat. Panic is stinging the back of my throat. Before I can object, he says, "Hey, shhhh. Calm down." He puts his arms around my shoulders, and continues, "I can handle this. It's no big deal. I promise I'll wake you up if either of us can't handle it."

"What if I can't pump because it's only been ninety minutes since I fed her?"

"Would you prefer a short nap? Or do you want me to go buy some formula?"

"I really want like eight hours uninterrupted." I feel guilty saying it out loud. Good mothers don't complain about the lack of sleep.

I'm about to take back the sentiment when Clayton says, "Your wish is my command. I'm going to go grab some formula that's good for sensitive tummies and some of those gas drops in case she doesn't handle formula well. Don't worry, she'll still nurse. Most babies do fine with a bit of supplement."

"Let me give you some money, at least."

"Nonsense. I didn't get to give you a baby gift. Let me do this."

I rub at my eyes with the heels of my hands and slide down on the couch until I'm laying down in the fetal position. "Clayton, how do you know so much about babies?"

He laughs. "I already told you. I've been around. Plus, my best friend from high school and his girlfriend had a baby before I moved away from Gulf Shores. My friend was freaked out, and I learned all I could to help out."

My heart softens as I consider what kind of person he must be to care for a friend so much. "Oh, that makes sense."

"You stay right here, and I'll be right back."

He slides forward to stand, but I grab him. "I needed to talk to you."

He kisses my forehead and says, "Well, just like you can't talk to me when I'm drinking, I can't talk to you when you're sleep deprived. Let's get this all sorted out, and we'll talk later."

His rationale sounds so awesome. The sheer joy and promise of a nap is too enticing. And I can't hold back more yawns. I yawn so hard my jaw hurts and tears fill my eyes. Wiping away tears, I say, "Okay. Take my keys so you don't have to knock."

Clayton is gone and I'm passed out on the couch in the blink of an eye. When I finally surface again, he's got Lyric in his arms. They're swaying and she's gumming away on a bottle of formula. I have to cover my eyes as the sun is low enough in the sky that it's coming in through the back door. "What time is it?" I ask as I stretch.

He steps backward into the kitchen to glance at the microwave clock. "A few minutes past three."

Shocked, I stand up. "P.M.? What? I've been asleep all day. Why didn't you wake me up?"

"Hey, hey, take a deep breath," he says, walking toward me. "She's fine. I've been feeding and changing her. She's napped some, too. It's only been a few hours. No big deal, okay?"

I know he's trying to calm me down, but I can't help feeling like I've abandoned her. "My first job as mom, and I failed her."

He chuckles. "You haven't failed her. You can't be a good mother when you neglect yourself. Try to sit back down and let me finish feeding her. When she goes back down, we'll have that talk. Okay? Do you want to hold her? Will that make you feel better?"

I shake my head. Clayton's voice is so calming and peaceful. Lyric seems to be happy with him. He's managed to ease my panic a bit. "You're doing a really good job at that, you know."

He smiles and continues swaying my baby. When she finishes the bottle, he swoops his head to move the floppy brown hair that's dangling over his brow, then skillfully moves Lyric to his shoulder to get her to burp. When she does, it's no baby burp. She full-on, grown-man, burps. I'm, frankly, impressed. Clayton seems impressed, too. I can tell by the crazy look he gives me. It's a facial high-five with his mouth wide open and eyes the size of dinner plates. It's as if we've witnessed the greatest thing on Earth. Maybe we have. This whole baby thing is pretty freaking amazing. More so, I'm impressed with Clayton's ability to care for her.

"In my experience," Clayton whispers, "there are always two burps."

Shrugging, I ask, "Even when there's one *that* big?"

"Always. Wait for it." He assures me knowingly and continues bouncing her, patting her back as he hums. And he's right, the second burp is tiny, but audible nonetheless.

"You know babies," I say as I wink at him. Where I had doubts earlier, I'm fully convinced now.

He cradles Lyric as he continues his bounce, sway, baby-rocking technique. I watch as he works her into a deep sleep and then takes her into the nursery. I reach over and switch on the baby monitor that's sitting on the end table. My heart thuds harder as I listen to him humming. Then I hear her signature, sleepy grunting.

Standing, I stretch some more and walk into the kitchen. I pull bacon, eggs, and everything else I need to make some breakfast. Then I start a pot of coffee. I switch on the tiny radio I keep in the kitchen and tune it to the oldies station, but keep the volume low. It takes a few seconds, but I finally get it dialed in as clear as possible. This station is playing Nina Simone, a song I recall my mama being partial to, "Take Care of Business." I start to sashay around the kitchen while the bacon cooks. I'm adding eggs to a bowl for some scrambled eggs with cheese. Setting the bowl down on the counter, I spin around to check on the coffee and Clayton has taken a seat at the table.

He's staring at me, smiling like a goof. "Nice moves," he jokes. "Breakfast?"

I frown. "Stop it. And why not breakfast?"

"I love breakfast. I can eat it any time of day. And why? I like it. Dance some more," he says, standing and walking toward me.

"Clayton." It's an admonishment that seems to miss its mark because he's not deterred. He walks like a man on a mission.

Standing still, I lean against the counter and shake my head. When he reaches me, I place my hand on the middle of his chest. "Clayton, stop."

He sighs. "I'll stop after this one thing. Promise."

"What do you mean 'one thing?'" I think I know, but I'm nervous. Butterflies are taking flight inside my chest and stomach.

125

"Something I should have done the day I realized I didn't want to just be your friend. You need to be kissed. You need to be kissed thoroughly. I knew it should be me, and I hesitated." He leans in to kiss me.

I side-step away from him. "No. You can't kiss me until I tell you everything I need to tell you. I have to come clean."

He holds up his hands in surrender. "Okay. Come clean." He backs away from me and slowly lowers himself into a chair.

"Coffee?" I offer.

He shakes his head. "Whatever it is, Melody, get it over with." His goofy smile is gone. A look of concern is creasing his brow.

I return to the stove and finish making us some food. I plate eggs and bacon for both of us and walk over to the table. I set a plate down in front of Clayton, then set down my own plate. Without making eye contact, I return to the kitchen for two cups and the pot of coffee. He watches me but doesn't speak.

I'm not sure where to start, but I know I need to tell him everything. If I want anything to come of a relationship with him, I can't do the same thing I did with Ryan. I'm not sure I want a relationship at all right now, but I know what not to do this time. My affair with Ryan was good for a life lesson, after all.

I drink some coffee, look up at him, and take a deep breath. "I didn't tell you the whole story about the baby's dad. I didn't tell you because it was an affair. He was married. When you said you couldn't tolerate cheaters, I thought you wouldn't want to be around me anymore. Not even as friends." I stop to let him process what I've said.

Clayton nods encouragingly, "Okay. Go on."

I take a moment to gather my thoughts. The honesty of looking him in the eye for this conversation is too much. My heart is aching, so I look down at my eggs and move them around the plate while I go on. "His name was Ryan. When he told me that he was married and how unhappy they both were, I thought I could get him to choose me over his wife."

I look up briefly to gauge his reaction, but he's not showing any emotions. If he's feeling something, he's not giving it away outwardly. I look down again. "I didn't call it off when I found out about her. I should have. I know that now. I was just selfish. I had this naive belief that he loved me more and that I could make him happy. It should be enough to pick me over her."

"Hey." His voice is soft. "Look at me."

I shake my head. "No. Let me finish."

"Melody." His voice is calm and insistent. Slowly, I lift my head and make eye contact with him. I was right not to look. He's not judging me as I expected. No, this is worse. His eyes are tender. Tears well up in my eyes.

He breaks the silence first. "Did you get pregnant on purpose?"

I shake my head again. "No. That was an accident. But once it happened, I did try to use the baby to force him to pick me. I'll regret that for the rest of my life."

"Why? What happened?"

"He died. It was an accident on the way out of town. He was headed toward my dorms. You see, I was in school at the time. We fought on the phone that day, and I hadn't told him about the baby yet. He was calling to break a date with me because his wife made plans."

I shake my head as Clayton takes my hand. He gives it a gentle squeeze as I rush through the rest of the story. "We fought because I felt like I was losing my grip. The idea of not having him, and having a baby on my own, was more than I could bear. I stupidly chose that moment to act like a spoiled brat. I threw the news of the baby at him. It wasn't fair. And then he died."

He moves his chair closer to me and releases my hand as he wraps his arms around me. He doesn't speak.

His silence is killing me. I shrug out of his arms and wipe at the tears trickling down my cheeks. "I'm not proud of what I did. I'm not proud of the affair. Lyric is the only thing I can be proud of from the whole situation. And despite my worst fear, I did have her. Alone."

Clayton doesn't say anything. He pulls his plate to him and starts eating the eggs and bacon I made him. After a few bites, he asks, "Her name is Lyric?"

I'm confused. Of all the things he could have taken from that confession, he asks about her name. "It is," I answer. "Her name is Lyric Jane. I named her for my mama."

"Is Lyric or Jane for your mama?"

"Both. Sort of. My mama was Jane, but she was a huge fan of music. She was especially fond of the Beatles." I pause. "Clayton, you're taking this extremely well. I confessed that I'm a lying, cheating, spoiled brat. Did you hear any of it?"

He smiles that trademark Clayton smile and strokes his beard. "What? Did you think I would be angry with you about your past?"

"Kind of. Yes. I thought you would be furious." I'm almost frustrated that he doesn't seem upset.

He shakes his head. "You didn't cheat. He did. That was his marriage vow to uphold. Sure, you made some bad decisions, but I think you were probably in too deep at that point. Everyone makes mistakes, Melody. You wouldn't be crying and confessing like a criminal if you were truly a cheater at heart. You actually feel bad about it. Most cheaters don't, in my experience."

Stunned, all I can say is, "What?"

"You've been dreading telling me all this. You've been beating yourself up this entire pregnancy, haven't you? It's why you kicked me out when you were in labor. Isn't it?"

I frown. "You've got it all figured out, huh?"

He looks like he's pieced something new together. "Well, no. Maybe. No."

I take the offensive position. "What if I kicked you out because you were suffocating me? You were hanging out with me all the time and helping me during labor. It's weird, Clayton."

"It's not weird. Friends help friends," he says defensively.

I smile wryly. "Oh, they do? Even in intimate situations like childbirth? There are parts of my body you've never seen, and you weren't about to see them like that! I don't think so. Weirdo." I walk to the sink and drop my plate in and start running water over the remnants of food.

He comes up behind me and slides his arms around my waist. He leans down to whisper in my ear, "What would you say if I said I don't want to be friends anymore?"

The warmth of his body against mine is all consuming. I lean back into him as I swallow, hard. "I would say, 'Whatever.'"

His hands slide to my hips. "I don't think that's what you'd say, Melody."

I turn to look at him. He's inches from my face, so I push up on my tiptoes as I put my arms around his neck. "You're right. I'd say you have to woo me. I'm no foregone conclusion." Then I put my hand flat on his chest. When I see him swallow hard and move his gaze from my hands to my eyes, I push him away. "You have to work for it, Clayton."

"That," he starts with a cocky smile developing on his face, "is doable. I will win you over. Let's come up with a plan."

Challenging me is the best way to get me excited about something. I don't know how he has me pegged so well. "Deal. What are the stakes? What's the challenge? How do we know who wins?"

He tugs me closer to him. "You will love me, Melody. Those are the only stakes, and we are both winners."

I swat at his arms. "Don't be cheesy. Come on. How do you plan to woo me? Because I deserve to be wooed."

He thinks for a moment and says, "Three dates. By the third date, you will be in love with me."

"You know I have six weeks of recovery ahead of me. So don't think about sex. That's not going to happen."

His dark eyes roam all over me. "I can woo you without sex. You'll be begging for it by the time these three dates are done. Just don't think it will be quick. When I decide to woo you properly, it's a process. You better be in for the long haul."

His idea sounds fantastic, and I actually love that he doubts my ability to go the distance. I let it sink in for a few moments. Three dates and I will love him. I like the idea of making him work for it. I'll never tell him the effort is unnecessary. It's an indulgent feeling to stand here letting him hold me and make promises of wooing. I deserve woo. I deserve for someone to try and win my heart instead of my giving away everything I am from the get-go.

Clayton is willing to work for me. For us. I'm in an 'us' now. A package deal. The idea fills my heart with joy.

Chapter 10

The First Date

It's nearly six weeks since Clayton pledged to woo me in my kitchen. We spend Tuesdays and Thursdays together each week. I feel like I'm hanging on the ledge of a cliff waiting for this promised wooing, but nothing ever happens. We are like an elderly couple. He rocks Lyric and takes her from me every chance he gets. He says it's to give me a break. I'm almost resentful of my daughter for the attention she gets from him that I don't.

It's irrational. She's a baby, and I am the one that demanded he woo me. Our deal is my fault. If I wanted to push things and end the deal, I'm sure I could. Part of me is curious about what he constitutes as wooing. Despite my growing frustrations with waiting, the anticipation is quite delicious. Clayton is loving every moment of the tease as well. He makes a face or starts a sentence, and as soon as I engage in the conversation and start to think this is it, it's not. He laughs at me a lot.

Still, he has been the most consistent person in my life outside of Sunny and Anna. He has continued doing home improvement projects around the house. Mostly outside. Last week, he reset some of my fence posts that had become so degraded by weather that they wouldn't hold the panels up anymore. Usually his bursts of DIY work come after we spend some time alone together. I think he's sexually frustrated. But that's my game: he's holding out on the first date plan, and I'm holding out on kissing him.

As I'm thinking over the recent weeks with Clayton, and folding Lyric's laundry, the front door swings open. My guest is no surprise. It's Mrs. Irma. She's always been welcome to walk in as she'd like. Plus, she knows the baby's schedule and doesn't interrupt it.

I wave as she comes around the corner. She's moving slower these days. She can't make it all the way to the couch, so she sits at the kitchen table.

I meet her there and place my arm around her for a quick hug. "What's wrong?"

She shakes her head, and with no breath in her voice she says, "It's nothing, baby. Nothing at all."

"You're lying. I'm going to let you have it for now, but you will come clean with me soon."

Irma chuckles at me. "Whatever you want to believe. Get me some water, Mel."

I do as she asks, and as I'm helping her to get a drink, Clayton steps through the front door. Irma won't let anyone see her weaknesses. It's not in her. As Clayton says hello to both of us, she takes the glass from my hand and says, "Mornin', Clay. What brings ya by today? What lie did you make up to have an excuse to spend time with Melody?"

Clayton and I exchange a glance. He knows something's wrong. We both know, yet we're both afraid of upsetting Irma so we don't say anything. Always a good sport, he says, "You're onto me, Irma. I have no reason to be here except I'm going to woo Melody one day. But first, I'm going to give you a hug and check on Lyric."

After he hugs Irma, he steps over to me for a hug. I whisper in his ear, "She's weaker every time I see her lately." I have to choke back unexpected tears as I say it. "I'm worried."

His answer is a nod. "We'll talk later. I have some thoughts."

While he looks in on Lyric, I sit with Irma. "Tell me what's going on. Did you see the doctor yet?"

Irma sighs and rests her elbows on the table. "I did. It's not great news for the world, but its good ta me. I didn't come to tell you all of that today. I came over ta ask if you have taken the baby to see your daddy yet. Have ya?"

"You know I don't have a relationship with my dad. I don't know if I can go see him."

Irma clicks her tongue at me. "Stop making excuses. Sunny and Anna told ya he's doing better about his drinking. I don't know why, but I have a conviction in my soul that ya need ta get yourself over ta see him before something happens an' you lose your chance. Don't be a hard-headed fool, Mel."

I don't want to see him. I want to rebel and tell her she's crazy. Irma is waiting for me to respond. "But I don't..." I can't finish making another excuse before Irma is fussing at me again.

"No excuses. Ya do as yer told, hear?"

Clayton comes into the room. "Who's making excuses, Irma?"

She smiles up at him. "Dis girl you care so much about has a bad habit of making excuses when it comes to dealing with her daddy and findin' forgiveness. Maybe you'll help her with that. Now, ya take this old lady home. I'm tired."

I'm filled with awe as I watch Clayton help Irma to her feet and aid her to the car. She apparently walked down here, which would explain why she's so tired. Still, the fact that she's tired from a walk she's made nearly every day is alarming to me. *Why is she so tired all of a sudden?*

I'm sure without asking that Clayton will come back after he drops her off, so I start a pot of chili for dinner. I've come to learn that Clayton is a meat fan and a fan of my chili. It's nothing spectacular. A basic recipe of ground beef, tomato paste, beans, water and spices. I don't think it would ever win any cook-offs.

He's being kind to keep me cooking for him, I'm sure.

By the time I close the lid on the slow cooker and start the timer, Clayton is back. His face is white as a ghost as he comes through the front door. "We need to call her grandson. Didn't you say you know him?"

I nod. "I do. His wife, Rhae, gave me this house. Before we call anyone, what's going on?"

He shakes his head. "I don't know for sure, but she's got that look about her. It's the same look both of my grandparents had before they passed. Her family needs to be here."

"Irma told me she was sick but didn't seem worried. I don't want to upset Rhae and Cade if I don't have to."

Clayton hugs me, and I can tell he's scared. Really scared. "You need to call them. Please. For me."

I do as he asks and call Cade. I do it on speakerphone, after some preliminaries and niceties, Clayton says what he observed. He has such a dude way of talking that Cade doesn't seem disturbed by his news. He says, "Thanks, man. I'll see y'all later this week."

~

We spend the day in our typical routine of playing with Lyric, eating some dinner, and finally watching a movie after she goes down for the night. The best thing about the last six weeks is that Ms. Lyric figured out that she would like more than two hours of sleep at night, too. This has been a much more agreeable situation for us both.

During a lull in the movie, Clayton whispers to me, "Let's take that first date."

He's surprised me because, at this point, I had assumed he was all talk and we'd never take that first date in which he promised to woo me. I sit up and let his arm slide off my shoulder as I turn to him. After a few seconds, he pauses the movie. "I'm ready if you are. Do you still want to be wooed?"

A huge grin breaks across my face. "Of course I do. I thought you had decided I wasn't worth the effort."

"Not a chance! You are worth it, and by the time I'm done, you won't ever doubt that again."

I'm so excited that I lean down and kiss him. It's a quick peck, but when I pull back, his mouth is hanging open and his eyes are huge.

"Melody, you just kissed me. Are you feeling okay?"

I grin. "Asshole. Don't make fun of me."

"Oh, I'm not making fun. I'm seriously concerned. I thought I'd have to work harder at getting to that point with you. I'm glad you're easy."

I smack his arm as he leans in toward me. "I won't kiss you again until you earn it. I am not easy."

He laughs as he pins me on the couch. "I know you're not,

but I do want to kiss you again.

I stroke his beard as I say, "Ha! Well, that was all you're getting until I see what this date is all about. I told you once before, and I'll tell you again, I'm worth wooing."

"Fair enough. I'll pick you up tomorrow for lunch. I'm bringing the babysitter." He finally lets me go so he can leave.

He's standing by the door, putting on his coat when I sit up and start to whine about him not finishing the movie. His face is full of mischief when he says, "I can't sit on this couch snuggled up watching a movie for a second longer. It's killing me to want you all the while knowing that we have a deal. I have work to do. Later."

His departure leaves me feeling bereft. There's a chill in the space he had been occupying. I want him back immediately, but I'm too stubborn to call him.

~

I spend the next morning getting Lyric bathed, fed, and dressed. She's playing in her crib while I knock out my own shower. I have become pretty quick at showering and getting ready within the time she can be entertained by her mobile and lovies.

By noon, there's a knock at the door. I walk to the door grumbling about the games he's playing. He doesn't have to knock. When I swing the door open, it's Jess. I throw my arms around her neck. "When Clayton said he was bringing the babysitter, I didn't know he meant you!"

Her answer is as enthusiastic. "Imagine my surprise when he told me you were willing to let someone else keep Lyric! I'm glad to be here. I've been waiting for this opportunity for, like, forever. So, you have a date, huh?"

I can feel the heat in my face as I blush. "It's pretty silly, isn't it?"

"Not at all. Why would you think it's silly to have a date?"

I shrug. "Because I'm a mom now. I shouldn't be thinking about dating. You know, this is ridiculous. I'm going to call him and end this now."

Jess frowns and grabs my arm. "Don't you do that! Being a mom has nothing to do with dating. You have the most responsible sitter in the history of the world to watch her." She gestures to herself as she rants. "You are entitled to take some time off here and there. Don't let mom-guilt get to you. At six weeks in, if you cave to the guilt, you won't make it much longer as a mom."

I groan. "Ugh! You're right. How do I look?"

As she's answering me, there's another knock on the door. I ask Jess to answer it while I grab Lyric for her. As I come back in the room with my sweet girl cradled in my arms, Clayton is standing by the door with a bouquet of wildflowers. My heart flips as Jess comes to take the baby from me. I blink several times before my mouth dries up. "Hi."

Clayton returns my greeting with a shy smile. "Hi."

Jess clears her throat. "No instructions necessary. I have your number, Anna's number, and Irma's number. I know who to call and in what order."

"But what if..."

She gives me what I'm sure is her mom face. It's not a look I can argue with. "No what if. Have a great time. Clayton, get her out of here."

I waver, deciding what to do. Finally, I kiss Lyric's forehead and tell her I love her as Clayton lays the flowers down on the kitchen table. He opens the door for me and leads me to his truck. Once inside, he says, "Buckle up."

I have no idea where we're going, but the afternoon sun is warm and makes me feel brand new to ride with the wind in my hair. Every now and then Clayton looks at me. When I catch him, his smile broadens.

"Be careful, Clay. You might get stuck like that," I warn him.

"It'd be an honor to be stuck this happy."

I shake my head. "You certainly know all the right things to say, sir."

He doesn't answer, but keeps driving. After a long ride down some back roads, he comes to a field, but we don't stop there. He takes a small dirt road that leads to the back of the field

141

and parks us under a grove of trees. Then he carefully helps me get out of the truck and leads me a little ways into the grove. When we come to a stop, we are under the shade of old oak trees alongside a creek. He's definitely been putting in some work because there is an old quilt spread on the ground where he has also setup a small picnic basket.

"While this is certainly romantic, I must say it's a bit cliché. Picnic in the woods as a first date is kind of overplayed."

He gives me that sly grin I love. "Well, have you ever been on a picnic in the woods with me?"

"Feeling a bit smug there, aren't ya?"

"You demanded woo, and you are ruining it. Have a seat." He says this last part with a flourish as he indicates the blanket.

He's right. I'm ruining all of his efforts. So I take a seat and slip off my canvas sneakers. Clayton opens the picnic basket and passes me a Yoo-hoo. I haven't had one since I was, like, five. I immediately start laughing.

"That is certainly a romantic selection, Clayton."

He returns my broad smile with one of his own. "Thanks. Sunny said they were your favorite. I spent a good bit of time with Sunny these last few weeks trying to learn as much as possible about you."

"Is that so? What else did Sunny tell you?"

"Wouldn't you like to know?"

I decide to call his bluff. "Better not be anything embarrassing. If so, it's all lies."

He laughs. "You love strawberries, dill pickle chips, and red velvet cupcakes. Although, I'm a fan of strawberries as well." He opens the basket and takes out a container of strawberries. "I'm not sure I can get down with dill pickle chips."

"Try them together," I challenge. "They are both tart, but the sweet juices of the strawberry offset the dill pickle flavor."

"Sunny said you might say that. So, I got these, too." He turns and pulls out a bag of dill pickle chips.

I take on a serious look and then grab a strawberry. After I take a bite of it, I eat a dill pickle chip. The crunch and the tart are amazing and remind me so much of the days I spent on my parents' front porch. "Your turn," I say.

Clayton repeats the method I used to consume two of my favorite foods that seem completely at odds with each other. He looks like he might be enjoying it, and then he starts sputtering and spits it out. His face is priceless, and the bits of chip are stuck in his beard. I'm laughing so hard I start tearing up. He's still spitting and digging for a drink of his own to clear his mouth. He's not amused when he says, "That's funny, huh?"

"Oh, it's more than funny! I'll admit the combination isn't for everyone."

When he's fully recovered from the experience of my favorite foods, Clayton changes the subject. "Tell me about your parents."

I shake my head. "No."

"Why not?"

"Because it's not pretty, and I'm not sure you need to know all about me yet."

"What if I told you that Sunny already told me a little bit."

I shrug and look away from him. "Whatever he told you is all you need to know right now."

"Why are you afraid to tell me about them?"

I look at him. He's being serious. "You might decide I'm too damaged."

He scoots closer to me. "I promise there's nothing you can tell me about you that would make me think you're too damaged. We all have shit in our past that we're dealing with. You already told me about Lyric's father. It can't be more than that."

I consider what he's saying, and he's gracious enough to give me a little while to think before pushing me any further. When I finally get my thoughts together, I decide to tell him everything. It feels good to spill the secrets I've kept inside for so long. He is a great listener. I don't mean great as in he inserts an understanding sound every now and then. He's quiet. He nods. He doesn't speak. He lets me talk freely until the light through the trees starts dimming. I finish by saying, "That's when Sunny and Anna started taking care of us. They are my parents in any real sense of the word."

Clayton remains quiet for a while longer. Then he pulls me to him. He holds me, and I let him. He smells of sandalwood, and the way he makes me feel when he's holding me is intoxicating. I turn my head into his throat and his beard tickles my face. I reach up and run my hand over the beard. Its soft, and I think it might be my second favorite thing about his face.

I pull back and look at him, "Now would be a good time for a first kiss, Clayton."

I read every emotion he's having in his eyes. Finally, his face becomes intense as his eyes hood. He stares back into my eyes before taking my face in his hands. Slowly he leans into me. I lift my chin as I offer my mouth to him. He stops short of contact, and I can feel his breath on my lips. "Are you sure?"

I nod as I give him my breathless answer, "Yes."

His kiss is feather-light and gentle. Just the barest of contact. I push in closer to deepen the kiss as he pulls me into him. We are acting in concert with each other. I part my lips as his tongue gently slips between. I meet every taste he takes with a taste of my own. Clayton slides his hands up through my hair and cups the back of my head as he lays me down on the blanket. I shift, making room for him beside me. The stiffness of his movements as I run my hands over his arms makes the think he's holding back, and I take it as a challenge to push him over the edge.

He knows what I'm about, though. He reads my every move and finally breaks the kiss. Clayton is panting when he says, "I should take you home. Now."

While I'm disappointed he's not going to give into me immediately, I'm satisfied with the knowledge of how close he was to taking me. This might be an even more interesting game now that I know he wants me physically.

I help him pack up all of the picnic settings, but he refuses to let me carry anything back to the truck. He manages it on his own. As he slides into the driver's seat beside me, he clears his throat. "So, tell me about your dad."

I think it over before answering. "No."

He blows out a breath. "Look, Irma wants me to work on you about forgiving your dad. How can I do what she asks if I don't know anything about why she wants you to forgive him?

"Of course Irma's meddling again." Frustration laces my words.

"When will you be ready?"

I shrug and stare out the window. "I don't know. Maybe never."

"Is it because you don't trust me?"

I turn to face him. "That's not it. It's not about you."

"Okay. So try me. You've been wrong about my reaction to things before. Recently, even."

My laugh is humorless. "Fine. In simplest terms, my dad is a drunk. He's been worthless and completely incapacitated by alcohol since I was a kid. So much so, I don't even know how Mama got pregnant with my twin brothers. He tried to get clean a few times. He's currently a resident at Pathways. The state home for addicts and repeat offenders. Happy?"

He's quiet and still for a while. I fold my arms, satisfied that my summary of the situation was shocking enough for him to let it go.

"Why can't you forgive him?"

I groan. "Because it's his fault. Mama died. I was fifteen years old and left to raise twin baby boys. Anna and Sunny tried to adopt us, but I didn't want that. So they helped me any way I would let them. He damn sure wasn't capable of helping. Still isn't."

"Do you ever think that he's really sick? What if it was cancer instead of alcoholism?"

I scoff. "There's no comparison. I recognize that addiction is a sickness. He refuses to do what's necessary to be in our lives."

He takes my hand off the seat and kisses my knuckles. "I can't tell you what to do, but I think you should probably let go of some anger before it consumes you, too. Maybe you have an addiction to your anger about it."

I'm stunned silent. I open my mouth to respond ten different times and can't even start the argument. By the time

147

we're home, I jump out of the truck and head up my front steps without waiting for Clayton to open the door.

As I'm fiddling with my keys, he comes up behind me. "Melody, don't be angry with me. I'm trying to help."

I whirl on him. "I don't need help with that situation. Have a great night."

His face falls as his mouth drops open. "That's it? Goodnight?"

I step through the door, close it behind me, and then lock it.

Chapter 11

Goodbyes

For the first time since Lyric was born, I've allowed Anna to take her for the evening. Clayton and I had many phone conversations over the weeks following our first date. It ended with me angry and Clayton hurt. In the end, I had to admit that I over-reacted. He was gracious and didn't gloat. He's infuriatingly patient with me.

Many evenings we have dinner and watch a movie after Lyric goes down. However, with her at Anna's tonight, I'm hoping to ignite a fire between us. Our first kiss was magical, and I've desperately tried to bait him into a heavier make-out session. The man has the principles and morals of a saint. He refuses to give into anything. We kiss, we pet, get to second base and leave third completely available. And that's it. Every night we spend together has been like a re-run of my favorite TV show.

Tonight, however, I think I might be able to overcome his

objections. My plan is to be naked when he arrives. There's no way he can say no to that. Step one of the plan is to take a long soaking bath. A bath is a luxury I haven't indulged in since I was about four months pregnant. That's when the doctor suggested that I not soak in very hot water. I still don't' know all of the reasons I wasn't supposed to do that. I slide into the water, take a deep breath, and let the aromas of the bath bomb I was given at the baby shower permeate my mind. It's a chamomile and lavender bath bomb, and it is perfect.

"Mel? You here?" Clayton says as he's walking through the house. That's something else that's become all too common. He does that thing where he knocks as he's walking through the front door.

I don't answer him at first. When his footsteps are near the bathroom door, I call out, "In here." I purposely timed my bath for when he said he'd be here. I might be playing a little dirty at this dating game. It's been over a year since I had sex, and now that the hormones of pregnancy are vacating my system, I am feeling the need for a bit more than kissing.

Clayton stops outside the tiny bathroom door. He must be thinking of what to say or do next because he doesn't knock, he doesn't open the door, and he doesn't say anything. He simply stands there.

"Open the door, Clayton," I call out to him.

He coughs nervously. "Can't do that, Mel."

He's playing with me now. So again I call out, "Open the door."

Another person is in the hall with Clayton. "Melody? It's Rhae. We just got in. Do you think you'll be long?"

I scramble and water sloshes over the side of the bathtub. "Uh, uh... no. One minute. I'm finishing up." I answer as I panic to let the water out and get up without slipping. I'm thoroughly embarrassed at my brazenness. *What was I thinking? Oh my God.*

I hurriedly dress in sweatpants and an old T-shirt before wrapping my hair in a towel and heading into the living room. Sure enough, Rhae and Cade are sitting having a chat with Clayton. I step over to Rhae and give her a hug. "Hey. When did you get here?"

"A little bit ago. We came straight here. Clayton was pulling up at the same time we were. He let us in. I hope you don't mind."

"No, no, it's fine. Have you checked on Irma yet?"

"Well, we were hoping you could fill us in before we go over there. I don't want to upset her, ya know?"

"Of course." I start telling them how she's getting thoroughly exhausted by walking down to check on me. How she's trying to hide the fact that she's not feeling good. I explain how she said the doctor gave her news she wouldn't share with me yet.

"That sounds like my grandmother, all right," Cade says as he sighs. His face is pensive. "Thanks for calling us, Mel. I know she helps with the baby, but we feel a whole hell of a lot better knowing that you're here to look out for her."

I smile. "We mutually look out for each other. I need her as much as she needs me."

Cade and Rhae are going to stay with Irma at her house for a week. They are going to make up a story about Cade's business in Memphis needing him for a little bit. Irma will see straight through it, but I hope she lets them stay for a while. She hasn't been looking or feeling good for a long time.

After they leave, Clayton motions for me to join him on the couch. "Where's Lyric?"

I smile and snuggle into the crook of his arm. "With Anna for a sleepover."

"She's only eight weeks old. Do you think she's ready for a sleepover?"

I shrug. "Some Neanderthal of a man encouraged me to let her have formula, so it's been easier to let others help me with her. She's in good hands with Anna."

He tugs the towel off of my head and plants a kiss on my wet hair. "What scent is that?"

"Chamomile and lavender," I answer as I turn my face toward him.

His eyes become narrow slits when he says, "Was that a setup?"

I feign ignorance. "A setup? I was only taking a bath, Clay."

"You happened to take a long bath around the time you told me to be here. Sure."

"Well. Maybe it was. I didn't expect you to have company, though."

"Did you really want me to come into the bathroom with you?"

"Of course I did." My answer is matter of fact. Clayton stands and starts pacing the living room.

"I, uh, I..." he's stammering. "I'm trying to do this the right way, Melody. Don't do that anymore. I only have so much strength. Neither of us wants to give in so soon."

"Maybe I do. It's been a long time. I'm human, and I have needs." The begging in my voice is humiliating. It sounds so much worse out in the open than it did in my head. I instantly regret saying it.

Clayton stops pacing and kneels before me on the floor, taking my hands in his. "Don't break me, Melody. Let's keep our deal. It will mean more to both of us, I'm sure. Three dates. Three."

Hurt mixes with frustration at my need for him. I'm disappointed, and it makes me angry. I stand and drop his hands.

"We have a date nearly every night of the week! You are always here for dinner. We always watch a movie, and you always put Lyric to bed for me. If we aren't dating what do you call it?" I'm practically yelling at the end of my rant.

He calmly stands and walks toward the door. "I'll see you tomorrow when you've calmed down. I won't fight with you." He leaves. The headlights of his truck shine through the front door as he backs out of my driveway.

I stand in the middle of my living room and cry. My baby isn't here for a distraction, and now, I don't even have Clayton to keep me company. Fitfully, I swipe at the tears on my face and make a decision not to be angry with him. Instead, I go to bed.

~

The morning comes and it's been a rough night. I didn't sleep. I kept thinking over Clayton's departure and seeing his deep brown eyes in my mind. He cares about me for real. This isn't a game to him, and he's not giving in to being horny. Can't say the same for myself. I sit in my bed thinking until the sun is fully coming through the window. I check the time and then take a shower to deal with the knots in my hair developed through a restless night.

Satisfied that it's an appropriate time of morning, I walk down to Mrs. Irma's house. Rhae answers the door. She's smiling, but her eyes are puffy.

"What's wrong?" I ask as I step inside the door and hug

her to me.

Her body collapses as she sobs. "Irma. She's very sick." It's all she can manage for a few minutes. I lead her to the sofa and sit down with her in my arms. I let her cry it out until she can speak again. When she does, she pulls away from me and starts dabbing at her eyes with a tissue. "It's cancer. Lung cancer. She doesn't want anyone to know."

"Oh honey. I knew it was something bad. I had no idea how bad. What does the doctor say?"

Rhae sniffles. "It's stage four. He wants to do a combination of chemotherapy and radiation."

I nod, knowing where this is going from her reaction as she explains it. "Irma doesn't want treatment," I say so she doesn't have to.

Rhae doesn't answer. Instead, Cade comes into the room and sits beside his wife. "You know my grandmother is set in her ways. She says that at her age she'd rather have five great days than five okay years. She also asked that we not tell her adopted babies yet."

Confused, I ask, "Adopted babies?"

Rhae smiles. "People she has taken as her own even though they aren't hers by blood. You, me, and some of my friends like Alana and Jess."

Cade hugs Rhae and says to both of us, "Let's give her the

best days we can."

In light of the news about Mrs. Irma, I don't even think about how upset I am with Clayton for the rest of the day. I spend it with Cade and Rhae, deciding how to make her last days special. We include Lyric in our plans because she knew from the day we met that I was having a girl. I never believed in her sight until the day I gave birth. Rhae calls on some of her friends, and we plan to have a gathering at Irma's house so she doesn't have to leave home.

My first call is to Clayton, but he doesn't answer. Fearing he's upset with me, I send a text message: *Irma has lung cancer. We're planning a get together at her house to cheer her up. Will you come?*

I send the same message to Anna. She replies immediately that she and Lyric would love to be there. I put my phone away and start helping Rhae with the house while Cade runs to the grocery store. He said Irma makes the best jambalaya he's ever had, and she gave him a list. Irma would like to make the main entrée for her own get together. That is classic Irma, and it makes me want to cry. Rhae and I have decided that we are done crying. We aren't allowed to cry at all around Irma. We are both saving our tears for in case she passes.

People start arriving not long after we sent out the invitations by text. Jess and her family, Anna and Sunny with Lyric in tow, and some of Irma's church friends. As we are sitting down to eat, there's a tentative knock on the front door. Cade answers while we wait for him to return so that Irma can pray over the food. Joy fills my heart when Clayton steps into the room. He stops by Mrs. Irma's chair and kisses her on top of the head.

"Sorry I'm late, Mrs. Irma."

"You gon' be more than sorry if you don't sit down next to my sweet Melody."

Each person at the table laughs as they move to different chairs until the chair next to me is free. Anna has Lyric on her knee, letting her mash a teething biscuit. Clayton reaches for her and she squeals with delight as she reaches for back for him. I'm fairly certain my heart can't take anymore conflicting emotions today. I'm heartbroken over Irma, and the pieces are held back together seeing how my baby loves Clayton.

He's gentle as he holds her over his head and lowers her repeatedly for smacking kisses on her baby cheeks. Finally, he sits next to me. He kisses my forehead as he bounces Lyric on his knee. My face hurts from smiling at them. I'm on the verge of launching into an apology for ambushing him and getting frustrated. He notices and says, "Shhh. We're good. Let's enjoy this party."

Irma quiets the chatter around the table when she stands and says, "If Clayton is done interrupting, I'm gon' say grace now. Y'all bow."

We all diligently observe grace with Irma and then enjoy her jambalaya.

Clayton holds my elbow as we walk away from Irma's grave. It's been three days since her dinner party. When Cade said she had days, he meant it. I know that it wasn't just Cade that knew how long she had, Irma did, too. Some might question her decision not to take treatment, but not me. Those days were filled with love, and she was fully aware the whole time. She had the opportunity to say the things she needed to say to those she needed to say it to. Not like when my mama passed. We were all left feeling bereft. She left us without a goodbye. Well, I got a goodbye, sort of. She held my hand and said she loved me right before she left the world.

Even when I don't want to think about it, that scene plays over and over in my mind. Especially at a time when we've said goodbye to one of the best women I have ever had the pleasure to know. She was a rock. She loved us more than anyone could ever return. The world is a colder place because she is gone, but it is also redeemable in that we know how to love the way she did.

"Are you okay?" Clayton asks as I wipe the tears from my eyes.

I nod because I can't form the words to tell him everything I want to say at this moment. The words seem inadequate for the gravity of the day. Irma could have taken the treatments and lasted another year, maybe. But she would have been terribly sick and miserable. Cancer is a horrific disease on its own, and the treatments always seem to make it worse. Anna told me more than a few times about friends she watched go through the process.

Death is just more peaceful when someone has accepted it as his or her time. Mrs. Irma lived a grand life with her husband, and she felt a hole in her days without him. As Cade told us, "She has joined her greatest love in their peaceful forever."

After the services, we all return to Irma's house. Cade, Rhae, and some of his cousins are receiving friends and church members. Anna, Clayton and I keep ourselves busy directing traffic, cooking and cleaning. Sunny took Lyric home for a nap at my house. She had been passed around so much that she was getting sore. I could tell because she really didn't want anyone to hold her except Sunny.

When the last guest leaves and Rhae collapses onto the couch, we excuse ourselves. Cade walks us out and thanks each of us profusely. Anna, being properly raised and cut from the same cloth as Irma, promises to return the next morning to start on the packing for them.

"Anna, you don't have to do that. Cade and I can take care of it," Rhae argues.

I hold up my hand to quiet Rhae before she gets the full explanation of why Anna is going to help without permission. "Just let her help. She won't rest if you don't."

When we're done, Anna hugs me and says she's headed home. "Send Sun along when you get to your house, baby."

Clayton drives me home and walks me to the door. He stops before coming in. I'm stunned by this move. "Don't you want to come in?"

He shrugs. "I want to be sure you want me to come in, first."

"Don't be silly. I'm not mad at you. Come on in and say goodnight to Sunny."

"I'm going to go home and get rested up for work tomorrow. Tell Sunny I said goodnight." He smiles and turns to leave.

I want to stop him, but I'm too tired to sit up all night talking about feelings. He'll be back and we'll all feel better after some rest. I wake up Sunny when I put my keys on the nail by the door. He stumbles out of the chair.

"Hey, baby. Lyric has been down for a couple hours, I guess. You okay? Need anything before I go?"

I smile and hug him. "No. Anna went home already. She asked me to send you directly there."

His rough chuckle is comforting. "No worries about that. I need a good long nap. See you later, hon."

When Sunny leaves, I pull out my phone as I lock the house up. I text Clayton.

I think we need to start over. That first date was amazing, and I feel like we got a little sideways. I'll take all the blame for that. I tried to move us forward too fast. I'm holding you to our deal. Two more dates, mister."

I'm surprised at his quick response. *Agreed. I share the blame with you. Two more dates.*

I hesitate before I respond. *I want to go see my dad. I want you to meet him.*

His answering text is sweet. *I would love that.*

It's a huge step for me to want to take anyone to meet my dad. I'm not sure how I plan to handle seeing him. Maybe Clayton will make that easier; he makes everything easier. I daydream about having a relationship as wonderful and touching as Irma had with her husband. It's more than just a girlish wish or hope. With the things I've been through in the last few years, I'm sure of what I need my forever to look like.

If we don't work out, I'm going to swear off romance and relationships until the end of my days.

MEG FARRELL

Chapter 12

Second Date

Clayton and I have only talked by phone or text for about a month. I've spent my time helping Anna, Rhae and Cade pack Irma's house, have a yard sale, and get the house on the market. It was a rewarding and devastating experience. Her life was amazing. I know why she felt so easy with her decision to skip treatment. It's a powerful reminder of what's important that I needed in my life.

Rhae and Cade went back to New Orleans a few days ago. Lyric has kept me busy with teething and another growth spurt, which changed all of her routines. It has been an adjustment for both of us. She's growing quickly. Every day she's a little bit different from the day before. I work hard to take notes in a daily journal about how she's changing and how I feel about things. It's been a great outlet to sort out how I feel about Clayton, too.

He's been absent lately. I spend a lot of time thinking

about what I might have done to scare him away. The reality is that just being who I am and any number of things could have sent him running for the hills. I wouldn't blame him for being scared of taking on someone like me. There's a lot of baggage to deal with.

Sunny asked me to come back to work since the fall semester is getting ready to start, which means big business from college kids again. Anna has agreed to be my nighttime sitter. She comes over when I leave for work and goes home every morning when I get back. Luckily, Sunny has last call around three a.m., so I'm in the bed by five a.m. every day. It's been an exhausting pace with a four-month-old, but we're settling in again.

I usually spend at least one of my three days off catching up on sleep. Lyric doesn't particularly enjoy the hours I keep, so Jess takes her on that day. I honestly don't know what I would do as a single parent without all the hands I have to call on. Today is that day. I'm looking forward to a diving into a deep coma.

Jess arrives right on time. She and I discuss what the plans are with Lyric and her kids for the day. She's taking everyone to the zoo and out for lunch. It's a treat for her kids for doing well in school. I remind her that we haven't tried strawberries with Lyric yet and don't need to accidentally discover allergies with an emergency room visit. I offer Jess some money to help with the admission, but she refuses. As she always does.

I'm waving goodbye and blowing kisses to Jess and Lyric when Clayton texts me. I open it after they disappear down the street.

I know you plan to use today to sleep. I hope it's everything you want it to be. Tomorrow, when you wake up, can I take you on our second date?

I grin to myself as I answer. *New phone. Who's this?*

His response makes it clear that my humor has fallen flat. *It's Clayton.*

I'm glad I'm alone with this text message because I laugh too hard at his innocent answer. *Yes, I know. I was playing with you. Where are we going?*

I watch the little bubbles on the screen that let me know he's typing. It seems like he's writing a message, erasing it, and writing more. When I get anxious with waiting, his brief message comes through. *Oh! Haha. Something physical but fun. Be prepared. I'd recommend jeans and a T-shirt. Maybe some socks.*

I stare at the message, trying to figure out what he's getting at. Confused, I give up and respond. *Okay. That's cryptic, but I'm down. Let's see what ya got.*

With that somewhat settled, and satisfied that I haven't totally irritated him, I'm overcome with exhaustion. I should be able to get a pretty good nap.

~

I wake up the next morning and spend the early part of my day enjoying coffee and bacon. My favorite thing and the cheapest thing I can keep in the house on a regular basis. I'm going to have to find some supplemental income, though. My finances aren't where they need to be to support a baby. Sunny and I have spent a little bit of time discussing whether or not I can stay at the bar if I find a regular day job. I'm flipping through the classifieds in the free paper that comes every Tuesday, but the jobs listed are slim pickings. Whereas I used to wait tables by day and bartend at night, I don't think that's possible while I'm raising a baby. I would never see her.

I'm just short of freaking out with the lack of possibilities when Clayton texts a time for our date. I'm excited, but apprehensive. We haven't spent any time together since Irma's funeral, and I'm worried about what he's come up with as our second date. He's given me two hours to get ready. And reflecting on the physical aspect of his description has me concerned.

I put my coffee cup in the sink and run a bit of water in it and head to my bedroom to start getting ready. With a sigh, I lay out the outfit I want to wear. The T-shirt is an old high school drama shirt. It's white with a huge pair of red lips.

The drama club had an after-hours, off campus performance of *The Rocky Horror Picture Show* every year. Our drama teacher couldn't sanction it or participate due to the fact that we live in the south and the conservatives would have had her fired for it. At least she was convinced it would be a problem. I'm sure there are more closet supporters than she would have thought.

The only support I could offer was to show up, and my senior year I bought this T-shirt. I always felt like it was a shame that they had to hide this show because it was awesome!

I take a shower and put my long blonde hair up in high ponytail, leaving the ends to sweep the tops of my shoulders. The red lipstick I pick matches the red canvas sneakers I love and the lips on the shirt perfectly. When I finish my makeup, I make kissy faces in the mirror.

"Uh, you ready?"

"Shit!" I jump and grab at my heart. "What are you doing sneaking up on me?"

Clayton laughs. "Do you do that every time you wear makeup?"

I shrug. "That's none of your business. Besides, I haven't worn makeup since I've met you. I quit when the pregnancy gave me hot flashes and I would sweat it all off. Where are we going anyway? Should I rethink the makeup?"

His smile is childlike when he says, "You'll see. And no. I love the red lips. Adore them."

The grin that spreads across my face is involuntary. I instantly feel my cheeks heat. I want to press him for details just so he can keep telling me how much he appreciates the red lipstick, but I've decided to try and stop getting in the way. I intend to let him romance me as I requested.

We drive into Memphis, and I'm starting to think he's going to take me on a walk across one of the bridges. I imagine it'll be the new pedestrian bridge that has LED lights. They seem to dance as they reflect off the water. I'm excited just thinking about the lights they showed on the news. It would be romantic. I'm smiling when he takes an exit I don't expect. Moments later, we're pulling into the parking lot of a skating rink. I look at him, suspiciously. "Skating?"

"You don't know how to skate?"

"I know how. Do you know how?"

Clayton chuckles as he gets out of the truck. Before I can open my door, he's at my side holding a hand out for me. I disembark from the truck, and he tucks my hand into the bend of his arm. *Such the gentleman.*

Inside, he pays for our admission and our skates. This place is packed! There are kids of every age and even senior citizens skating. It's a cosmic skate night. The lights are lowered and the black lights are glowing. Some jam skaters roll by us in perfect step with each other. It's not a skill I ever had, but I wish I did. They look like they were made to be on wheels. Just the way they flow is impressive.

I can't help feeling giddy as we take the floor. Clayton holds onto me for dear life. I giggle like a little girl. The feeling of skating with him is exhilarating. My heart hammers in my chest and my face hurts from smiling. Clayton is not as skilled at skating. I feel terrible for leaving him behind struggling. It's absolutely beyond miserable when I see him wipe out with the small children on frames passing him.

As I come around, he's getting back on his feet, and his face is set in determination. He doesn't notice me because he's staring at his feet. I chuckle at the concentration he's putting into this. The music is loud, and I know he won't be able to hear me. I slide up to him and grab his hands. Clayton's shoulders relax as they drop away from his ears. He's tense from his fingers all the way up. I shake his arms to help him relax a bit more.

When he looks into my eyes, heat washes over me. He seems to enjoy holding my hands as we skate. I help him step off the rink and inch toward the carpet covered mushroom-like seats to rest a bit.

He's yelling when he leans over to say, "That shirt looks great under black lights. It's almost as if you knew where I was taking you tonight."

I wink. "How would I have known where we were going? Who else did you tell?"

He smiles conspiratorially. "Sunny."

"You scoundrels have become quite close, haven't you? Spend a lot of time talking about me, do you?"

He shrugs. "There's a lot to learn. Are you ready to go? We've been here about an hour and I'm worried I'm going to break something."

"One more time around for good measure," I say.

He nods. "I'm sitting this one out."

I laugh as I take off for the floor. I skate one lap as fast as I can manage in my out-of-shape state and decide on one last lap. I'm digging into a turn, crossing right over left, when a small girl on a frame pulls out in front of me. I can't remember how to stop fast enough not to take her out. There's people all around me, and I go down as I I'm trying to find myself an out. I put my arm down to break my fall, but I hit hard anyway. This is a bad thing to do, and I know it when I do it. My body just reacted out of habit.

I'm sitting on the floor, stunned. Clayton comes running up in his white socks, "Mel, are you okay? That looked really bad."

I nod. "Yeah. Fine. We all have our turn to fall, ya know? That's skating."

He laughs at me, and it's a nervous laugh. "Right. Tough as nails. Nothing bothers you. Give me your hand, and we'll get you off the floor."

I reach for him, but a pain shoots up my arm. The pain is bad enough that it makes me catch my breath and wince. Cradling my arm, I start crying. "Something's wrong."

Clayton swears under his breath. "I knew it was bad when you went down. Hang on," he says as he comes behind me and lifts me under my arms. On my feet, he rolls me slowly to the floor exit. All the teenagers around the rink stare. He helps me take a seat on the bench lining this wall. Carefully, he slides the skates

170

off my feet. I watch as he collects his rentals and returns both pairs. He comes back and helps put my shoes on for me. I don't have to move because he's got it covered. It's lame that all I can do is hold my arm to me and wait for him to help.

We laugh as we walk to the truck, and he drives straight to the Urgent Care to get an x-ray. All I can think about the whole time is that I don't have insurance. I'm going to have to pay off the Lyric's delivery and now an Urgent Care visit.

Clayton interrupts my thoughts. "What are you smiling about? I didn't see them give you any pain medicine."

I smirk. "They didn't. I'm thinking about how I will never be out of debt again. I definitely don't have the money to pay for this."

As I'm explaining this to Clayton, the doctor walks in. "Good news. You aren't broken. Probably a deep bruise to the bone. Rest and ice. Watch out for little kids at the skating rink."

"Thanks, doc," Clayton says as the doctor hands him the papers and tells us we can leave.

After Clayton helps me down from the examination table, he scoops me into his arms and kisses me. This is different than every other kiss. There's an urgency to it. Clayton takes it deeper as he squeezes me to him in a bear hug. I have to pat him on the chest a few times so he'll let me get a breath.

When he eases his grip on me, I sigh and sway on my feet. "I think I could love you."

The heat and simultaneous joy that fills his eyes consumes me.

Quietly he says, "I know I could love you. I'm so sorry you got hurt tonight."

"It's not your fault. You wanted to leave, and I wanted another lap of greatness."

He continues staring into my eyes. No one has ever looked at me with such intensity. He's pouring all of the emotions he's been holding back directly into me. "You were amazing. Sunny said you loved to skate when you were younger. I thought it would be a good thing to do for our second date."

He shrugs before going on, "It seemed a better plan than sitting silently in a movie theater or going out for another picnic. We aren't terribly low on options for dates, but I'm running out of ideas. You're just...you're difficult. You know that?"

I laugh. "I'm difficult?"

He nods vehemently. "I never can decide what to do or say to you. I live perpetually perplexed." As if making up his mind, he glances off for a second, and then back to me. "That's it! I hadn't put a word to it before. But you perplex me."

I'm not sure what to say. I frown, "Is that a bad thing?"

Clayton lets out a nervous laugh that seems to expand once it's in the air. "Yes! And no. I don't know. I like that I can't seem to predict you, but I'll be damned if you don't pose new challenges every day as I think of ways to achieve woo-age."

"Clay, honey, I don't think woo-age is a word."

"See! That's what I mean. You're way smarter than I am."

I smile at him, because I'm fairly satisfied that I can make him feel this way. It's strange, but powerful. I've never believed I had the upper hand in any situation. Everything that has happened in my life has been beyond my control. Until now. "Kiss me again, Clayton."

He obliges in the most thorough manner yet.

Chapter 13

Grace

Clayton and I make plans for him to meet my dad. It's been years since I've seen him. The whole idea fills me with anxiety and apprehension. I feel so many different things when I consider taking my sweet baby and Clayton there. So many questions cross my mind: *Will he be proud of me? Do I care if he's proud? Does he remember losing Mom? Has he finally ruined his liver? Is he sick?* I'm surprised at how much I seem to care about him. It's a confusing ball of emotions.

Sunny has been doing a good job of keeping him updated on my life and how the boys are doing. He takes Dad pictures and newspaper clippings when their scout troop or ball team makes a headline. Thankfully, they haven't been arrested yet. The good ole boys that comprise the Bell Hills police department know that they don't mean any harm. They're just boys. Anna, however, holds them accountable for every flower they pick for her without permission. She truly makes them walk the line.

175

In preparation for our trip, I've packed the playpen, a snack bag for the road, and a small cooler of drinks—both water and formula. As I'm finalizing the outfits for Lyric's diaper bag, Clayton does his typical knock and enter. He yells out for me, and I call him into the nursery.

"Are we taking everything you have by the front door?"

I think for a moment. "Yes. It's everything we'll need for a full day on the road with a baby."

He groans. "She's not that needy."

I look at him sideways and prepare to argue. Before I can get really cranked up, he holds his hands up in surrender and backs out of the room.

With Lyric finally dressed, and her diaper bag ready, we head into the kitchen to wait for Clayton to get everything loaded. The drive to see my dad is three hours, one-way. We'll have to stop and change Lyric's diaper or give her a bottle at least once on the way there and once on the way back. I'm trying to be practical and have us home in time for her bath and bedtime routine. Anna is always fussing at me to keep her on routine. It's hard enough with the job that I work, a road trip notwithstanding.

"Hey, Sweetpea! You ready?" Clayton sounds so silly when he's talking to Lyric, and it melts my heart every freaking time.

As soon as she sees him, it becomes almost impossible for me to hold her. She squirms and squeals until he takes her from me. I've given up on being her favorite person if Clayton is around. I hand her over to him. "Why don't you get the air started in the truck and make sure she's buckled in securely."

"You got it, babe."

Deadpan, I ask, "Babe?" Just trying the word in my mouth feels odd but appropriate. I roll it around in my mind a few more times.

He chuckles, and without hesitation, he says, "Yep. Babe. C'mon, let's go. You can't keep stalling."

I nod. "All right. Why do you think I'm stalling?"

He shrugs. "Because this is going to be awkward and might hurt a little bit. You've avoided it for a long time. Take your pick."

I set my jaw in an obstinate manner and groan.

"Don't be mad. I'm here for you. Even if this sucks balls, I'm with you. We can keep this as short or as long as you want. If you want to leave as soon as we get there, we'll go. No pressure."

"Thank you. I guess? Watch your language around my baby."

He looks puzzled. "What did I say?"

"Sucks. Balls."

~

Lyric does great on her first road trip. She only needed one change on the way down. I'm sure that's my fault since I made sure she had a full bottle before Clayton picked us up. As we pull into the long driveway for   Pathways, identifiable by the chipped sign by the road, all the tension I'd been able to hold back fills my body. I'm stiff from the stress of thinking about what I'll say or what Dad might be like now.

Clayton reads me better than anyone ever has. He reaches for my hand and says, "You've got this."

I don't answer him because I'm afraid he'll see all too clearly how much I'm freaking out. Instead, I try to focus on the trees that line the drive up to the main facility. Both sides of the road have these huge, crooked trees that seem to reach for the cars that drive by. They are crooked with dense leaves that create an umbrella of shade. The purple azaleas planted around the bases of each are the only color until we reach the building at the center of the property. The building is more like an old antebellum home. The wide, wrap-around porch is lined with white rocking chairs and porch swings.

Clayton lets out a low whistle as it comes into view. "That is some place. Wow."

I'm in as much awe because I couldn't picture the building even though I've been down here a few times over the years. It's interesting what the mind can do with details when the body is panicked or upset about something.

As we park, I take a deep breath and ask Clayton to get Lyric out of her car seat for me. He snuggles her into his arms as I get the diaper bag. Everything else can wait until we need it. We walk up the steps together. Having him with me is helping to keep the anxiety about being here away. Again, he's making things better for me.

At the front desk, a sweet, southern lady asks how she can direct us.

"We're here to see Daniel Richards. Which room?"

The look on her face is tender. "You must be Melody."

I smile. "I am."

"Right this way, darlin'." She leads us down the hallway to a broad staircase. My Dad is on the second floor. She takes us down the corridor to the left, and leaves after instructing us that we'll find him in the second room from the end, on the right.

Clayton passes Lyric to me. "You go first. I'm right behind you."

With a sigh, I turn and walk toward my Dad's room. When we get there, he's seated in a chair by the window, looking out. I can somewhat see what has his attention. The view through the trees surrounding the property is serene, with the sun barely peeking through. As I'm stretching on my toes to see more, he turns to look at us.

"Hey, honey."

I freeze. It's my dad, but not as I remember him. I swallow hard and clear my throat so I can sound more sure of myself. "Hi, Daddy."

He waves us over. "Come and sit down. Let me see that

baby."

We take a seat across from him. His face is lined more than I remember, and his coloring is gaunt. The years of alcoholism has taken a toll on him. I'm instantly sad for him, for me, for the boys, and for Lyric. Most of all, I wish I could cry out to Mama. She would be distraught that he's this sick. As much as he made his choices, it was a burden that she carried. She wanted to be enough for him to keep him well. It just wasn't important to him.

"Can I hold my granddaughter?" His hands shake as he reaches for her.

"Of course."

Instead of passing her to him, I stand and set her on his lap. I don't let go until both of his arms encircle her. Even then, I stay close so if he's too weak to hold her very long, I can catch her.

His voice shakes when he asks, "What did you name her?"

I hesitate for a moment, unsure how to tell him her name. After a moment, I say, "Lyric."

He blinks up at me. "Lyric? Lyric what?"

"Lyric Jane Richards."

Tears fill his eyes and spill down his face as he looks into her cherubic face. Her cheeks are rosy and her skin is pale. The peach fuzz covering her head seems like it might turn out white-blonde like mine.

She's holding his skinny, crooked finger and cooing at him. "What a beautiful name for a beautiful girl."

Unable to bear the pain and tears, I turn away from him. Clayton is still standing in the door.

I smile in relief and hold out my hand for him to join us by the window. "Dad, I'd like you to meet someone else. This is Clayton."

Dad lifts his head to see Clayton. He swipes the tears from his face and gruffly says, "So this is the baby's daddy?"

The shift in his demeanor is quick and startling. I stumble for the right thing to say. "Ah, no. He's a..." I hadn't even thought about how to say who Clayton is to us. "He's... my friend."

Dad nods. "Hi, *friend*." The sarcasm on the word *friend* is palpable.

Clayton steps forward and offers his hand. "It's very nice to meet you, sir."

Dad doesn't return the gesture. He resumes his focus on Lyric who has started squirming to get to Clayton. He is her favorite person. Dad becomes hurt by this and offers her to Clayton before she can hurt herself.

We spend awhile chatting about Mama and how much he misses her. He asks us a little about the twins and Sunny. But his disposition never improves. In fact, I do most of the talking. He's begun slumping in his chair and not making eye contact.

I nervously glance between Dad and Clayton. Eventually, I back off of chatting and try to enjoy the view from his window. It is breathtaking. Probably the best part of the visit.

Dad never specifically asks how I'm doing or why I don't visit. He has lost interest in me and Lyric.

When the sun gets impossibly low in the sky, the lady we met at the front desk comes by the room.

"Mr. Richards, it's dinner time. Your family can wait in the dining hall while Charles gets you ready for dinner and games tonight."

I send Clayton ahead with Lyric and ask him to grab her formula in case she decides it's time to eat. As he's leaving Charles, a male nurse, comes in.

I greet him, "Hi there, I'm Mr. Richards daughter. Can I stay while you get him ready for the evening?"

His voice is scratchy but kind. "All I'm going to do is help him to the bathroom before dinner. We'll be down directly."

"Oh. Thank you. Can you or anyone fill me in on his health?"

Dad is downright angry when he says, "You care now?"

I glare at him. "I've always cared. You've made it impossible for me to be around you." My heart starts pounding in my ears. I'm trying to stay calm because there's clearly something

182

I don't know about his health.

"Bullshit. You should probably take your baby and baby daddy home, now. You've done your duty by checking on me. Don't get involved in my care. Go on with your life and leave me here to die. Charles will see to my body."

I'm floored. I look to Charles, who shrugs and leans closer to me as they head for the door. He whispers to me. It's a quick word. "Alzheimer's."

Fear and concern for my father are not something I expected from this visit. Irma knew. She and Sunny both knew. Of course they knew. They've been fussing at me to come visit and to find forgiveness for him. It makes sense, now.

I head down to the dining hall. Stunned, I take a seat next to Clayton.

He reaches over and pats me on the knee. "Are you okay? You're pale."

I shake my head. "Dad has Alzheimer's disease."

Clayton is silent but takes my hand. After a moment, he turns and kisses my temple. He's so gentle with me, and his soft beard always tickles my cheek when he does this. "What do you need me to do?"

"I don't know. What is there to do? I've never known someone with Alzheimer's. Upstairs, he basically turned on me. He became mean and spiteful. Charles told me about his diagnosis."

"Ah-ha."

I turn to look at him. "What does that mean?"

"I understand why he's in *this* facility." He stresses the word *this*. "Melody, this isn't a home for addiction and recovery. Haven't you noticed the other patients in here?"

I think for a moment. I haven't noticed anything. My own little bubble of emotions has consumed me. Cautiously, I start looking around the dining hall. There are so many elderly people here. They are all in various stages of ability or disability. Some are rocking, some are singing or humming, one lady is throwing the mashed potatoes from her plate to the floor. At the table closest to us, the nurses are helping their patients eat. It's devastating. At last, my eyes land back on Clayton who's looking at me tenderly. "Will this happen to my dad?" My voice is small and sounds scared. I am scared. I've been awful to him. He needed me, and I wasn't there for him. I'm torn by my anger for how he neglected us, but I did the same to him.

He shrugs. "Let's ask Charles when they get here."

As if summoned, Charles pushes my dad's wheelchair up to the table. "Mr. Richards, what do you think you want for dinner today?"

My dad is no longer grumpy. He's childlike when he says, "Macaroni."

I smile at the simplicity of the request. Charles says, "Good choice. Too bad it's what you want every night." His sense of humor must come from the frustrating behaviors of his patients. He locks the wheels on Dad's chair before walking into the kitchen attached to the dining hall.

We're all silent as we wait. I don't know what to say, Clayton is waiting for me to start, and I'm not sure if Dad is still aware that we're here. After a few minutes of uncomfortable silence, watching other families, Dad turns to me. His face lights up when he says, "Melody! When did you get here?"

My heart breaks. I smile. "We just got here, Daddy. Do you want to meet Lyric and Clayton?"

His face breaks into a broad smile. "Who are they?"

I begin introductions all over again. We have a nice dinner. Charles eats with us, and I get a chance to ask questions about Dad's condition. Charles has been a nurse in this facility for most of his career. He explains how Alzheimer's affects people differently.

In his experience, Dad is doing better than most. "I think it's because he's stubborn as hell. I like working with him because of that." He also tells us that Dad is one of two patients he's responsible for. It helps to have a low patient count for each caregiver because Alzheimer's is very unpredictable.

It gives me some comfort to know that Dad has a great caregiver.

We say our goodbyes when Charles indicates it's time for Dad's bedtime routine. Before we go, Charles hands me his business card so I can call to check on Dad whenever I want.

~

We arrive back home well into the evening. Lyric has slept most of the way, which is new record for how long she can sleep. I rode most of the way in the middle of the bench seat in Clayton's truck. This allowed me to both snuggle with him and keep a better eye on Lyric. Her lengthy rest made me worry if she had stopped breathing once or twice.

Sitting close to Clayton is peaceful. He plays the radio low on a classic country station and hums along under his breath. His arm around my shoulders makes me feel more content than I have in years. My whole life has been spent in turmoil. Always waiting for the next bad thing to happen. And there has been no shortage of bad things. I smile to myself as I consider what it might be like to have a partner in life.

As I'm contemplating the possibilities, I turn my face to look at Clayton. When he looks at me, I smile.

"Hey, you," he says it quietly so he doesn't disturb Lyric.

"Hey," I whisper.

"What ya thinkin' about?" he drawls like a cowboy in a western.

I sigh. "Thinking about what life would be like with a

partner. To have someone who shares in the struggle."

Eyes back on the road, he grins. "Just playing devil's advocate here, but what if it was someone to share in all the sweetness life has to offer as well?"

It's something I never thought about before. The negative side of things is what I always wait for—the ways things can go wrong or someone could leave me. I'm living my life in anticipation of the tragedy.

"I've also been thinking about Dad. I don't know why I've held onto the bad feelings about him for so long. I think I made a mistake by holding that grudge."

He nods in agreement. "We all make mistakes. It's life. We're human, and whether we like it or not, we are emotional creatures. Based on everything you told me, as a kid, you didn't have a lot of guidance on how to handle what happened with your mom."

I lay my head on his shoulder. "I didn't let anyone help me either. I stayed angry and busy. I didn't want to deal with it. Anna and Sunny would have done anything to help me. They tried. I'm hard-headed."

He squeezes me closer. "You can't change anything about the past. You can only make decisions to improve the future. Teach Lyric better than that."

I smile and rest my hand on his tummy. We ride in silence for a few miles while I think about what he's said. As usual, he's right. I do spend a lot of time in the past, but I have this great little girl who's just starting out in life. She needs better coping skills. She needs to know how much she is loved and valued. She needs to know her worth. All of that will come from me.

"Clayton, I want to plan the third date?"

He laughs. "Well, that's unexpected. But, as you have pointed out before, we've had more than three dates. We spend nearly every night together."

"And," I say sarcastically. "You always remind me that we agreed on three dates. I've let you set two of them. I'm taking over for the third. You okay with that?"

He turns those big brown eyes on me for a moment and then focuses back on the road. Finally, he says, "Okay, Mel. You set the third date. But I warn you—it better be amazing. You have big shoes to fill. I set the bar pretty high."

"Challenge accepted."

Chapter 14

Third Date

Nearly two weeks have passed since we took a trip to see my dad. Things have been hectic. Lyric got her six-month shots, which made her violently ill. I have learned all the Mama techniques for handling fevers and the knots that can develop at the injection sites. This round was so hard on her I think I honestly cried more than she did.

As I'm laying Lyric down for a nap, I hear the front door open. I run for the door as soon as I can, thinking that Clayton has finally come to visit. When I get there, my shoulders sag because it's just Sunny.

He laughs when he sees my face. "I'm glad to see you, too, kiddo."

"Sorry. Thought you were someone else."

"Uh huh. How long has it been since you saw him?"

"Forever. It feels like forever, anyway. Probably not as long as I think."

Sunny scrunches up his face. "Why so long?"

I shrug. "He's busy. Said he had to go out of town for some emergency. He texts me sometimes, but I haven't seen him. It's making me crazy."

Sunny laughs at me. "Whatever, girl. He'll be back around. You have him strung out pretty bad. It makes me nervous that he's so soft."

I roll my eyes. "What brings you by this fine afternoon?"

As I finish my question, Anna walks through the door. "Oh! Hey, honey."

I hug her. "What's going on? I don't usually get both of you at the same time."

Anna smiles. "Well, we just wanted to talk to you about your dad. We haven't been straight with you about his condition, and I wanted to apologize to you. You probably would have been to see him sooner if you knew."

Sunny wraps an arm around Anna because he can tell she's getting upset. "It's my fault. I told her that he had put you through enough and that you didn't need the guilt of dealing with his issues.

I love them so much that the blame game is frustrating me. "Y'all need to stop right there. I'm an adult. I could have asked at any time. Sunny, you told me to go see him. Begged me, even. Irma told me to find forgiveness for him. What I decided to do then or now, is on me. I do have questions, though. I was processing all of my feelings about it before I brought it up with you."

Anna offers to make some coffee as Sunny and I settle at my tiny kitchen table. "When was he diagnosed?"

Sunny is shifty when he answers, "I don't know. Maybe five years ago. Early on, they thought he had dementia. It wasn't until he got to Pathways that the specialists there called it Alzheimer's."

"What is the prognosis?"

Anna joins us at the table as she says, "It's not good, baby. It's different for everyone, but for your Dad to reach this state in five years means his is aggressive."

I nod, understanding what they mean now that I've seen the mood shifts first-hand. "Is it because of his problems?"

They exchange a glance, but Sunny is the one who answers, "Most likely. The studies on Alzheimer's have different opinions. More believe that alcoholism can cause the brain damage that leads to both Dementia and Alzheimer's."

I take a deep breath, preparing myself for the one question I'm scared to ask. "What should I do for him?"

Anna reaches across the table and takes my hand. For the

first time, I realize that she's been aging all this time, too. Her skin is as paper thin as I recall Mrs. Irma's being. I've been taking her for granted all this time. I vow to pay closer attention to her. I don't want her to get sick and slip away from me, too.

She looks me straight in the eye. "You can't do anything for him. Not really. What I want you to do is for you. You need to go back to see him. I want you to tell him that you forgive him. Forgive him for your mama. Forgive him for the twins. Most of all, forgive him for not being the Daddy you needed."

Tears are spilling down my cheeks. I wipe at them furiously because I thought I was done crying over him.

Before I can say anything, Sunny takes over. "Forgive him for yourself. Lyric needs her mama to be whole and healthy. Holding grudges ain't healthy for nobody, baby."

Instead of talking anymore, I cry. I let the grudge I've been holding go. The peace I've needed fills the spaces left vacant by the anger I've been holding on to for so long. Anna wraps me up in a large hug that only she can give.

We spend a while longer talking about all the great things that have been happening to me in the last year. It's something I haven't done enough of, lately.

When I lost Ryan, I allowed the anger for my dad and the loss of him fill me in ways that I shouldn't have allowed. I gave power to all the things that should have been temporary. No more. I won't give any more energy to people and situations that haven't earned it. The first thing I'm going to do is finalize how I feel for Clayton.

I look at my adopted parents and the way they smile at each other, and how they gravitate to each other. I don't even think they know they do it. They must touch or look at each other at all times. There is an invisible rubber band around them that expands and contracts, but never breaks.

Inspired, I ask Anna and Sunny for some assistance with the third date that I took away from Clayton. He was reluctant to give up control, especially since he had taken on the challenge of romancing me. I realized on the road trip with him that I may be deserving of woo, but he is, too.

Anna and Sunny leave after we discuss my plan, and then I text Clayton.

Will you meet me at Sunny's bar tomorrow night? 7:30?

My nerves crawl under my skin and make me nauseated as I wait for his response. Thankfully, he responds quickly. *Of course! I should be back tonight and free tomorrow. Is everything okay?*

I can't help the way I feel in this moment as I reply. *Perfect.*

~

As I sit in the floor playing with Lyric, I'm anxious and excited about today. Clayton and I will have a firm direction at the conclusion of our third date. Three dates were all he said he needed to make me love him. I think he underestimated his skills. That, or I overestimated the challenge I could pose to his abilities.

I chuckle out loud and Lyric turns to look at me over her shoulder. My heart melts at the sight of her smile. A wide, rosy, smile that shows off her first four teeth. Her innocent giggle simply in answer to my own laugh reminds me of how lucky I am to have her. Things could have turned out so different, but God had a plan.

We're both distracted when there's a knock at the door. I stand and make my way over to unlock and answer it. Jess is standing on the other side with a large cup of coffee from my favorite local shop.

"Oh! You are a lifesaver. I didn't even know I wanted that, but I do!"

Jess laughs at me. "You are an addict, sweetheart. What are we doing this morning?"

I grin broadly. "I told Clayton that I was planning our third date."

She gasps. "No way! He's letting you?"

"He has no idea what he's in for. Come in, let me tell you my plan. I need help with the finer details."

~

Jess and I spend the bulk of the day running around town picking up what we need to pull of my master plan. Part of the scheme involves a list of people that I think need to be at the bar when Clayton arrives.

After she drops me off back at my house with the things we picked up today, she confirms her tasks with me. "So, I need to have tell everyone to be there by seven p.m., right?"

"Yes! Please don't forget anyone. They'll think I left them out on purpose. Anna is going to keep the baby, and she'll bring her when it's time."

Jess laughs at me. "I still can't believe you're doing this. It's crazy. Hope Sunny doesn't lose the bar over some child protective services call."

"Ha! Shows what you know, Jess. That will be a contributing to the delinquency of minors' issue. Not some lame CPS call. Duh!"

It's four-thirty, which gives me a little over two hours to get ready. There's so much to do that I'm on the verge of panic.

Before I get the chance, Clayton texts me. *I made it back to town. I have news for you. Can I come over?*

I respond quickly, *No! I'm working on the plans for our date tonight. Do. Not. Disturb.*

Melody, you know I'm a simple man. Please don't make some huge elaborate plan. I just want to be with you.

I'm smiling so big at his words that I cover my mouth with my hand. *I know, baby. I know. You are simple. That's why I love you. But you aren't planning this night. I am.* My reply is simple, *See you in a little bit.*

He doesn't text back, so I know he's respecting my plans for the evening. I resume my preparations by laying out the dress and boots I want to wear tonight. I've already put my hair up on fat rollers to give it some volume and a little swirl. It's far too long and heavy to sustain actual curls.

I pick up my guitar. Something I haven't done since before Lyric was born. Walking over to the chair in front of my full-length dressing mirror, I sit and pull the guitar in front of me.

At first, the sound is timid and unskilled. It takes a little while to reacquaint myself with the strings. My fingers are clumsy and weak. It takes a toll on the muscles in my hand to hold the strings down for the right chords.

I'm on the verge of tears as I keep practicing. Silently, I curse myself. Why didn't I make this plan for a few days from now to give myself time? But I take a few minutes break to pace the room and get my thoughts together. Calming breaths help. It also helps when I imagine the scene in my mind of how tonight will go. "Fortune favors the brave", my mama used to say. I don't know where she got that quote from, but I love it.

~

The time for Clayton to arrive has come. I'm backstage of the tiny platform that Sunny keeps for entertainment. He never has anyone willing to play the frat-boy scene that his bar frequently turns into. Plus, most people who are any good, prefer to play the bigger bars in Memphis. That's where the money is. Sunny's place is little more than a dive. Still, it's our place and I love it.

Jess did her job perfectly. People have been arriving for about an hour now. Trickling in one at a time, and now coming in groups of three or more. She's come back to bring me water and gossip about what's happening while I wait.

Anna has been trying to get details out of her, but Jess is a steel trap when she needs to be. No one is getting this plan out of her. Again, I'm thankful for having her in my life.

For all I went through with Ryan, there are some great people and things left because of that situation. That diving plan is something else. It still surprises me. I wonder if it always will.

I look down at my watch and force my feet to stay still until I think Clayton has arrived and settled in at the bar.

As I'm deciding to go out, I hear Jess take the microphone. "Hey, y'all! Quiet down. Listen up." She waits for the crowd to follow directions. "My friend Melody has asked you all to be here tonight because it is a special night for her and her sweet thing, Clayton."

The crowd erupts into whoops and laughter and my face heats. *I'm getting her.*

Jess is back on the microphone. "Clayton! Get your ass down here. Front and center!"

This is my cue. I step up on the stage. As I do, I spot Clayton standing down front. His face lights up when he sees me. I don't want to talk to him before I do what I came here to do.

He can't help himself, so he mouths, "I love that dress."

I nod and hold my finger up to shush him.

The crowd starts laughing again.

Clayton takes a seat on the barstool that I'm sure Sunny or Jess put there for him.

As I place my guitar strap over my head and settle the guitar in front of me, I step up to the microphone on the stand. With a heavy sigh, I start playing. The song I selected for this moment is a song I used to sing with my mama on a regular basis. It was our song, and now it's *our* song—Clayton and I.

The tempo is slower than the original recording. "Happy Together" by the Turtles is still recognizable. I begin to sing with my eyes closed. By the time I reach the first chorus, I look directly at Clayton.

Despite his thick, dark beard, I can see the smile on his face. He's impressed. The thought gives me courage to continue. By the time I finish the song, the bar is singing with me. Many couples are wrapped in each other's arms, swaying and singing the sweet lyrics to each other. Jess has my baby on her hip, singing the words to her.

Tears prick my eyes. Once the song is finished, it's the right time to make my move. "You told me that I would love you. Our deal was for three dates. I planned to be a challenge to you so that I could keep you on your toes."

I smile at him, and take a step closer to the edge as I continue. "You see, I've been hurt a lot in life. I usually expect only terrible things to happen to me. Then there was you. Cocky, handsome, and infuriating. I mean, it probably was the pregnancy hormones. But you were undaunted. You were sure that you were someone that could love me."

I take one more step toward him. "I learned the hard way that you were right. You are someone I love. Not just possibly, not maybe, not one day—now."

I step closer and rotate my guitar behind my back. "So, Clayton, I want to know if you want a partner in life. If you would like someone to endure the struggle with you and rejoice in all the happiness life has to offer. "Can we be *happy together?*"

By the time I finish, his brown eyes are wet with tears he's trying to hold back. His smile is contagious, but he answers my question with a question. "What are you asking me, Melody?"

I roll my eyes and release the tension in my shoulders. "Well, dummy, I'm asking you to marry me. Will you?"

The tears are rolling down his face as he reaches for me. "Yes. Melody Richards, I will marry you. Where do I sign?"

I take off my guitar and hand it to Trey, Clayton's brother, who's standing beside the stage. Then I jump off the front, making it to Clayton in three long strides. I jump into his arms and wrap my legs around him, planting a kiss firmly on his mouth.

His hands grapple my ass as he struggles to regain his balance after I attacked him. But he kisses me fiercely as he spins me in circles. Both of us are crying happy tears in celebration of how we made it to this moment.

When I pull back, he says, "I told you that you would love me."

"Wait, what was your news?"

He chuckles. "Nothing compared to your epic third date!"

Epilogue

"Hey, babe. What are you doing out here?" Clayton sets down a glass of tea and takes the chair closest to me on the back porch.

I run a hand over my face and yawn. "Watching the fireflies try to outsmart our daughter."

He laughs. "She's something else. How's our boy doing?"

As if on cue, our son flips over in my belly and stretches. I groan and rub over the aching place where his foot seems to be. "I can't believe you talked me into doing this again. What was I thinking?"

His laugh is hearty. "I didn't talk you into it. You were blissed out and jumping my bones every chance you got. It's not my fault."

I gape at him. "Really? You weren't a willing participant?"

"Woah. Settle down. Don't bring out mean Melody. I don't like her. Plus, I have to keep you happy so you'll let me be there when he's born."

I wince. "Are you really going to hold that against me?"

He leans over and kisses me. "Only if you do it again."

I smack his arm. "You probably shouldn't stress the pregnant lady."

"Daddy! Don't be mean to Mama." Lyric runs up the steps to join us.

He turns. "Aw, punkin. I'm not being mean to Mama. I love her. Did you catch very many fireflies?"

She juts out her bottom lip. "No."

He lifts her up onto his lap. "Well, don't give up. You still have time. I'll help you."

Together, they run out to the gazebo under the shade tree and wait for the fireflies to come close.

I watch them play and remember the day we got married. When he officially became her Daddy.

I gave Jess and Anna a little over six months to get things together. It was everything I had dreamed it would be. My dress was gauzy and white. It flowed in the wind as I walked up the hill to meet Clayton in front of Trey, our officiant.

Trey figured out that he could pay seventy-five dollars to an online place and receive an ordainment which would allow him to perform weddings. No one gave Trey a second thought. Hell, I did everything out of order and that was the least offensive part of the ordeal.

I wore a ring of flowers in my hair while Lyric wore a pink

dress with tiny rosettes on her skirt and socks. The pink of her dress perfectly complimented the pink in her baby cheeks. Halfway through the brief ceremony, she started whining, and the only thing that would settle her down was Clayton.

We said our vows and exchanged rings while Clayton held our sweet girl.

It was a perfect day with an even more perfect evening.

After the reception, we left for New Orleans. It was my first time in the beautiful city. We spent time with Cade and Rhae. It was at dinner with them that Clayton finally got to deliver his news.

Cade needed a foreman for his Memphis construction business. Clayton was looking for a job that would allow him to support a family. He knew things would always be hard for us with him being a mechanic and my being a bartender. We weren't even together officially when he had started interviewing and training with Cade.

While I believed I had the upper hand with that night, it was always Clayton. He's always a few steps ahead of me. It was infuriating at first, but now I've come to appreciate how he thinks ahead. We still agree to discuss the big things.

That was four years ago. Life has never been more perfect. In hindsight, it all came together when and how it needed to. Irma was right to fuss at me so much about trusting in God and walking by faith.

Irma was fond of telling me, *"You must go through a test to have a testimony."* Boy, was she right.

About the Author

Meg Farrell was born and raised in Mississippi where she and her husband, Jason, still make their home. The Farrells have three children and a host of other non-human lifeforms.

Most of the time Meg can be found running between softball fields, hockey rinks, band concerts, and choir performances. Meg is an avid reader and enjoys books from nearly every genre.

Meg's books are available on Amazon for purchase as a paperback or e-book.

Learn more about Meg and how to connect with her on social media by going to http://www.farrellwrites.com .